HER VAMPIRE MASTER

MAREN SMITH

BURNING DESIRES

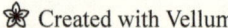 Created with Vellum

MIDNIGHT DOMS

*O*nce upon a time, we vampires lived on the horror of humans. We lived for the pain, the fear. That BDSM has come so openly to the world has given us an outlet to continue to feed in the manner that suits us best— sweetening the feast with every stroke and cry, our victims becoming supple and willing, well-marinated meals just waiting for that next bite to be taken. We no longer leave large body counts in our wake, but we aren't half as civilized as we like to appear.

We are the Midnight doms. At night, we hunt. At midnight, we feast. Be careful, little human, or you might become our chosen prey...

(EXCERPT ABOVE ADAPTED from <u>Her Vampire Master</u> by Maren Smith)

. . .

THANK you for picking up the first book in *Midnight Doms,* a spin-off of Renee Rose and Lee Savino's *Bad Boy Alpha* shifter series. Be sure to check out Alpha's Blood, the book that inspired the series, featuring Lucius, the vampire king.

We are so grateful to Maren Smith for agreeing to be part of this project and kicking it off with such aplomb!

Love and dominant vampires,

Renee and Lee

-JOIN OUR FACEBOOK PARTY ROOM: https://www.facebook.com/groups/701925946969115/

—SIGN up to get news of the Midnight Doms releases: https://www.subscribepage.com/midnightdoms

PROLOGUE

The Dream

*T*he *music in Club Toxic pounds.*

I'm dreaming, I know I'm dreaming, but the scene feels so real. I feel it the way my sister felt it, the reverberations moving up through the floor, making my already unsteady legs even more so. Thumping all the way into my head until the pulses aren't just in my ears, they're in my brain. In my veins. Pulsing along with the flashes of color that are either a strobing product of the DJ's light show or my own panicking brain. Like my sister, Jez, I've long since lost the ability to tell.

Stumbling with every step, I push through the crush of revelers. Those who can dance, are. Those who can't, still jump up and down, adding to the throb of the beat with the unified pulse of their combined weight hitting the flashing tile lights of the dance floor.

I spin around, searching the blur of their shadowy faces, shoving to break through the crowd and fighting to find a breath of cool air that doesn't reek of booze and hot bodies. The cooling fans blowing down from the ceiling are fighting to keep up, I can barely feel a whisper of air movement against the sweat on my face, and even those whispers felt hot.

As hot as his touch. I just have to find him first, and somehow convince him to make me his again. Because she needed him, and now I need him too.

I claw at my arms, nails digging in to soothe the unbearable itch that lives in my skin, but there's no relief, and my desperation ratchets higher, notch after notch, until finally I spot him. Dark, enigmatic. Black hair and black eyes. Beautiful as an angel, seductive as sin.

He's out on the floor, dancing at the center of this throbbing, pulsating crowd with a tall blonde woman almost as beautiful as he is.

My breath catches as I stare, mesmerized by the movements of their bodies. He holds her back to his chest. The tight skirt of her black mini dress is pulled all the way up around her hips and the hot pink band of her thong is nothing more than a twist of color around the tops of her thighs. One hand is on her throat, his other plays between her legs.

They could be fucking instead of dancing.

The way her ass grinds against his hips, they probably are.

I push through the crowd, fighting to make my way closer, coming right up to them. I see everything.

The pump of his pelvis against the naked flesh of the

blonde woman's ass. The circling, stroking motion of his hand between her milky thighs makes the bump and throb inside me melt down like summer's honey until the molten ache of it is centered, has its own special pulse, in the heaviness of my womb.

The other woman's eyes remain closed as her lips part. Her head drifts back against her seducer's shoulder and her blonde hair, streaked in highlights of pink and purple, stands out starkly against the black of his blazer jacket. Her thighs shake, the subtle movements of his fingers making her hips grind back in time. She pressed her hands flat against her thighs, because that's where he whispers for her to put them. I can hear his instructions echoing in my head. It's a game he has played with me—with Jez— every night in my dreams. No matter what he does or how badly she wants to, it seems she is not allowed to touch him without permission.

She is, however, allowed to come and judging by the constant quivering of her soft thighs, she's almost there.

He turns his face into her hair, caressing his lips along the heated slope of her neck, before, almost as if he senses me, the dark-haired man opens his eyes. He looks right at me, and smiles before stealing that first slow lick and taste of his partner's skin.

I tremble, the echoing caress of his tongue moving up my shoulder to my ear. I feel the rasp of it, the hunger of it, and the pain my sister felt at that man's complete lack of anything approaching apology or even sympathy. He kisses the blonde woman's neck and, hunger in his eyes, looks right at me as he bites.

My sister felt that bite all the way down into her clit,

which was exactly where he'd bitten her the first and last time he'd had her. I feel that bite the same way now, shaking up through my wobbly thighs as the ravages of the most intense orgasm rip through my itching, twitching, hungry body.

The hurt is more than just physical, because in the black of this beautiful man's eyes, I can find no remorse for what he's doing and nothing that might indicate he has any interest in doing this to me again.

This beautiful man.

This jaded man.

This man who had, before he'd ever touched Jez, told her plainly that he did not believe in love and had no interest in playing for keeps. He never plays with the same woman twice.

I know it, just like Jez knew it. But she'd wanted it, just like I want it now. It's a drug in our system. The itch that refuses to be assuaged no matter how desperately we scratch and claw, fingernails subconsciously raking down our arms until we're bleeding, trickling crimson streams that cut the paleness of our flesh until our blood drips to the floor.

He notices.

So do several others. Shadowy heads in this faceless sea of dancing, jumping, writhing strangers turn to look at me. Nostrils flare, hungry eyes lock on me from every direction as if my pain and need are something they can smell.

My only warning before my arms are seized is the tell-tale flick of that beautiful man's gaze shifting to something just behind me.

"You're done," the bouncer says, half dragging, half carrying me as I struggle and shout, stumbling over my own clumsy feet all the way to the door. He shoves me out into the cool embrace of night. "Go home."

The doorman refuses to let me back in after that. He even threatens to call the police, but the beautiful man can't stay in there forever. He finds me uncounted hours later, long after the muffled pulse of the nightclub music goes quiet and the lines of people waiting for access inside vanish. By then, I am huddled in the side alley, my back to the rough bricks, scratching at the unbearable itch in my arms and legs, and so sick now with my sister's need that I can't even throw up anymore.

Coming to me, he lowers himself to squat beside me. Gentle fingers peel back my eyelids as I whimper, "Please... please..."

His stare is pitiless, even as he softens enough to sigh, "You are almost more trouble than you're worth." His voice is every bit as beautiful as the rest of him. "Come along then."

My dream changes then. The nightclub is gone. So is the beautiful man. Instead, I see the sun coming up, chasing back the shadows and washing the dirty Tucson streets in splashes of orange light. It crawls over rooftops, up the old brick and crumbling adobe of derelict apartment complexes, and spills across the weed-choked cracks in the pavement of the abandoned parking lot where my sister's body lies nude among the bull thistles. Splashes of her blood dot the grass, and on the pale stretch of her broken neck are two needle-like puncture wounds.

Every night I have this dream. Sometimes I see more

than this, sometimes I see less. But every morning I wake up to certain details that never change. My sister, Jez Chapman, is dead, the police report reads prostitute, and the cause of death is overdose.

CHAPTER 1

 *erris*

I DON'T KNOW the name of the man who killed my sister, but I know his face. I see it in my dreams every night, exactly as it happened to Jez just before she died. He drugged her—they found the date rape drug, Rohypnol, and heroin in her system at the autopsy. He bled her—even had the heroin not been lethal, the quantity of blood absent in her veins was. He left her like garbage in the weeds— she's buried in Holy Hope Cemetery now, beside our parents. I bring them roses every Sunday.

He must have thought no one would notice now that she's gone. He must have thought no one loved her, but he could not have been more wrong. The police labeled her a prostitute. They say her death is drug-related, and they've stopped looking. But they're as wrong as he is, and I'm going to prove it. My name is Merris Chapman, and if it's the last thing I do, I'm going to find the man who haunts my dreams. He's going to pay for what he's done.

At the heart of every city, the crown of its nightlife is usually only worn by one place. In Tucson, that place used to be No Return, then it was Club Eclipse on Congress Street. But in the last year, it's become Club Toxic and it was one of Jez's favorite places to go. The line of hopefuls anxious for a chance to get in here always stretches around the block. Not everyone has to wait in line, however, and a girl's best chance of getting in doesn't even involve the doorman. I stood in line for hours twice before I figured it out. A short, tight dress and flawless makeup are all a pretty woman needs. I put my long brown hair up in curls atop my head and take a position up near the ropes, in full sight of those just stepping out of the backs of cabs or private cars—the ones who never had to wait in line. The beautiful people just walk past the doorman and go inside.

Sometimes they come with company. Sometimes they come alone, with a roving gaze over the hopefuls until they find something—some*one*—they like. The one who likes me came dressed in a tux with two women who could have been Hollywood movie stars clinging to his arms. Still, he pauses at the rope and gestures for more of us to follow him, and in we go just in time for the bar to close. He doesn't care that many of us stop following him the minute we're through the door.

I am one of two who immediately go a different way. I've never done anything like this before. This isn't my life. My twin sister, Jez, is—*was*—the rave, concert and party girl. I'm the quiet one. The one who likes to stay at home. I like books and music. I watch documentaries on *Discovery* and YouTube. I'm an artist. During the day, I design buildings for a prestigious architecture firm. In my off time, I like to draw scenery—forests, mountains, beaches with rolling waves that only I can hear crashing up against the shore in my head. I haven't been out of Tucson since I was a kid, when our parents took Jez and me to Yellowstone Park. That was the summer before they died, and after that, we were in foster care. Some siblings get lucky and are placed together in the same family. Jez and I weren't.

We were separated on our first night. Shortly after that is when I had my first Jez-dream. She'd fallen down the stairs at her new house, bumping her nose, chin and knee in her tumble down that short flight of carpeted steps. I felt every impact as if it had happened to me. That was the first time, but it was far from the last. That's how I know the interior of this place without ever having set foot inside it before.

I know the bartender's face—a redhead with a quick hand and a tired smile, and a voice that bellows out 'Last call' like an army drill sergeant. The black collar she wears doesn't mesh with her uniform, but it doesn't exactly stand out either. She's not the only one in a collar. Seems a weird fashion choice, considering the effort this place has gone through to make it seem high-class. Everyone is in uniforms. Even the bouncers and doormen dress in suits and ties. The cocktail waitresses bus through the crowd, making sure those at tables have everything they need, their tight black shorts showing more than a little cheek each time they bend over. Just a little too slutty to be classy, just a little too classy to be a brothel.

I get a drink so I won't stand out, a vodka strawberry lemonade. It's Jez's favorite, and the only one I know how to order because it's not like these places come with menus. Asking for one would definitely make me stand out.

Fighting back the *déjà vu*, I circle the room. It's all so foreign and so familiar. Weird things capture my attention and spike that feeling higher. This is the last place my sister was before she was killed. What am I looking for? I honestly don't know, but strange things catch my eye. Like the way flashes of light keep reflecting off the sign on the women's bathroom door, something Jez would have seen just before she pushed her way inside.

The same flashes spark back up off the dance floor tiles, polished to a mirror shine beneath the wildly prancing feet of all these people. I see the smiles, the laughing, the sweating... but I see them like I did when I dreamed it. Certain faces leap out at me. The two men standing guard at the coatroom door. The door is closed, but in my mind, I see the secret stairs leading down. *I feel the pressure on my hand as he takes it, the way his eyes glint back at me—my sister—as he draws her down.* Into what, I'm not sure. My dreams don't play like movies. There are no verified beginnings or endings. Just snippets of scenes all jumbled together, bits of a movie on the cutting room floor, waiting for me to put them back into an order that makes sense.

The music is loud. The bar might be shutting down, but the nightclub side of this place will party on for another two hours at least. This whole place throbs to the pulse of the bass. I dreamed that too. I dreamed the five-foot-nothing, dark-skinned beauty right now pinning her man against the wall in the shadows by the bathroom. In my dream, the man was Asian. Tonight, she has a taste for blonds, but her hold on his wrists is exactly the same and so is the sultry way she leans into him, the tip of her tongue flicking out to lick a sinuous path up the side of his neck. He laughs, nervous, breathless, thoroughly aroused. It's too loud in here for me to really hear it, but I heard it in my dreams and the echo of it is with me now.

I circle the dance floor, wending my way through the crowded fringes. I recognize one blonde waitress, that sexy uniform still so very tight on her voluptuous curves. In my dream, she's coy and smiling as she leads Jez to make an introduction. Her blue eyes lock on me just as we pass one another, and a shock of recognition flashes across her face, but I've already passed her. I'm in the lounge now, where the lighting is much dimmer, and the smell of alcohol and anticipation become thick and cloying. I've done and seen all of this before. The people, the tables, the couple in the corner with another woman backed against the wall, eyes closed in the sharpest of ecstasy as they both kiss on opposite sides of her neck, coaxing her to come with them someplace else. But in my mind, it's Jez's sigh I hear as a man's hand sweeps the hair from her neck before leaning in, close as a lover, the curve of his handsome mouth losing the sincerity of its smile as he leans in for a kiss.

I stop, frozen where I am. My eyes lock on a man holding court at the far table in Club Toxic's lounge.

I don't know his name, but I'll never forget his face.

MAREN SMITH

I see it every night in my dreams.

It's the man who murdered my sister, and God help me, but I see now why she went with him. The man is beyond handsome. Tall, athletic, with eyes as dark as his hair, a clean-shaven chin, and a smile that would make angels ache to sin.

They would have to get in line. He already has a woman on—not at—his table. Sitting in the center with her back to me, she leans back on her arms, her knees drawn up and legs spread impossibly wide. She has a lime wedge in her mouth, a shot glass on the table between her legs, and he's sprinkling salt on the very narrow patch of cotton that makes up the front of this woman's thong panties. It's a wonder the bouncers haven't asked them both to leave.

There is nothing in this man's movements that suggest he fears anything as he caresses his hands up the woman's legs to her knees—

...his hands caressing the straps of Jez's dress off her shoulders, baring her to the waist... I flinch from the vision in my head and stare at the man instead as he keeps the woman's legs splayed wide and bends to suck the salt off her panty-clad mound.

He spots me just before his mouth touches her, and he stops.

Do I look like I hate him? I try to mask how fiercely I do, but the instant absence of all expression on his face as he stares back at me is startling. This is the man who killed my sister, though I haven't any proof. If I want him to pay for what he's done, then somewhere deep inside me I have to find the courage to walk over there.

Finding him was only half the battle.

Now I have to get him to confess.

~

Aleron

SOMEONE SIRED a companion out of one of my past suppers.

That was my first thought, but even as the shock of what I'm seeing sings through my veins, I know what I'm looking at can't possibly be my needy little Jezebel. Jez is dead. Dead in ways not even we can come back from. I know because I went to the hospital to see her. After the way she was found, I had to be sure. Sadly, I did not arrive until well after her autopsy. I can only assume her body had already been released back to her family. All I could smell was the unmistakable odor of embalming fluid seeping from her pores.

I don't often pay attention to the passing of humans, but Jez was… different. Not special, not really. But considering how I left her and the state in which she was found, perhaps one might call it a needling sense of guilt pricking at my conscience for not insisting when she refused to let me take her home.

I'm not the only vampire who views Club Toxic as his own personal hunting ground, and Jez is—was—not the only unwitting victim here. She is, however, the only one I've personally known to pay with her life.

I didn't know Jez had a sister, much less a twin, but the longer I stare, the more certain I am that's what I'm seeing.

Her body and face are perfection. She is every bit as slim as Jez—small in waist and breasts, a little thicker in the hips and thighs. Curved instead of bony, exactly as I prefer. Even her golden-brown hair seems identical, pinned up as it is in curls atop her head. When released from that prison of bobby pins, I know the tresses will be just long enough to wrap around my capturing hand.

She's made up her face just like Jez would, but there the similarities end. Around the eyes... the shade of her lipstick—something isn't right. She has painted herself to be a seductress, but hers is an unpracticed hand.

Her mouth isn't smiling either. The piercing gray of her eyes is hard, holding no welcome for me.

No, this is not Jez. I am certain of it before I even test the air, picking my way through all the smells of this room until I find the alien allure of her scent.

I forget about my drink. I lose all interest in my date, although that's hardly new for me. My interest has been aggravatingly fickle for centuries now. Nothing holds it for long, but this... Oh now, this is holding it nicely. She's come for me, this lovely young woman with my Jezebel's face. She hates me too, something I find both curious and amusing. She's a puzzle.

I like puzzles; there are so few new ones left to excite me.

Sitting on the table between us, tonight's supper frowns. Following my stare, she glances once over her shoulder and then turns her pout back to me.

"Give me a few minutes," I say, patting her hip. "If you hurry, Izzy might yet pour you a drink. Tell her I said you could have anything and to put it on my tab."

My would-be supper is not mollified, but I have dangled the carrot that is me before her hungry eyes for a very long time now. She wants her night with me too much to blow it with a tantrum, although she is anything but gracious as she rolls off the table and stomps to the bar.

I've already forgotten her. Bring forth the puzzle. I beckon 'Jez' to me.

Mine is a small, round table surrounded by half-moon booth-style seating. I am in the center, with as little of the room hidden behind my back as possible and within each reach of anyone who might decide to sit with me. She doesn't look at all tempted by my offer, but she inches closer until she's standing before me. Her gaze doesn't leave mine; she barely blinks.

"Pretty as I am to look at, I doubt you came here simply to stare. Come," I invite again. This time, I even move, sliding left to give her as much room on the right of the booth so she'll feel safe and perhaps even think she's out of my reach. "I don't bite," I lie with a ready smile.

I can smell her reluctance. I can practically taste her anger. That it's directed at me is as obvious as it is baffling, but what I don't smell and don't taste is fear or lust, and oh, how that does enthrall me. It's been some time since anyone has approached me without exuding one of those two emotions. I am far from the oldest vampire... dare I say *alive*? But even so, one does not get to be as old as I without learning to read the human animal as easily as if it were a printed book. She's angry. She's hurt. She wears my Jez's face, and I'm not a fool.

I truly do love puzzles, so I'm quick to put these missing pieces back in their proper places. Her anger suggests she blames me for what happened to her sister, but if she knows me to be capable of murder, then her utter lack of fear is intriguing. Also, why me? She can't possibly have even the smallest clue who and what I am, or even as angry as she is, I doubt she'd approach me the way she has. She even sits down when I give the table a cajoling pat. No, she's not afraid of me at all.

I like that.

I also like her smell. Like her sister, her scent is attractive to me. She's never been here before, or I'd have known it. I'd like to think my eye would have picked her out before now. Her neck is fully exposed, and there are no healing marks that I can see. If someone else has supped from her, then they found another place to do it from, and my lazy cock stirs at the thought of where I might find the marks.

"Can I get you a drink?" I offer, flagging a club servant with a mostly empty tray. "Water? Coffee? The bar's closed, but I'm sure I can get you something."

"No," she says, slowly. "Thank you."

Angry, but still polite. Her voice isn't quite a mirror of Jez's, but it's very close. A little more alto, perhaps. A little huskier. A bedroom voice, they call it. Old and jaded I may be, but I'm not immune. Probably because I haven't yet fed tonight.

Over at the bar, my darling, sulky, thoroughly pissed-off ex-supper is just petty enough to turn her tasty flirtations on another vampire. I don't know his name, but he's only too happy to pick up where I left off.

He steals her away from the bar, throwing a smirk my

way. I can imagine what he whispers in her ear, as he leads her off in the direction of the Dungeon.

That's mildly annoying. My fingers drum the table once, but that's all right. I have my puzzle, and with all the willing meat to be found in this place, I doubt if I'll go hungry for long.

Answering my hail at last, a bar servant comes to my table. "We're past last call, Sir." She tries to keep her eyes properly averted, but her gaze keeps stealing back to my companion. I know what she's thinking. From the corner of my eye, I can see rumor spreading among the submissive cast. They recognize Jez. They can also read a paper every bit as well as I, but they aren't vampires. They don't know what I knew the minute I could smell her.

"Are you sure you don't want something?" I ask, but the waitress is already retreating, racing back to the bar to spread 'Jez's' miraculous resurrection tale into another corner of the room. I'm glimpsing discrete glances from other vampires now too. The rumor is spreading through the shadows like wildfire.

Lifting her hand, she puts the drink she's been carrying on the table between them. I haven't seen her take even the tiniest sip. If she really were Jez, last call or not, she'd have been on her third by now. That girl did so love her vodka.

"I have one," she says. "Thanks anyway."

Still polite, still with that glint of fury that her tattle-tale eyes cannot begin to hide. She's not clever in that way. She doesn't know how to lie.

Mayhap I should teach her. At the very least, I think, my puzzle and I should have a little fun.

Merris

HE STICKS his hand out as if to shake mine, and it's all I can do not to leap right over the top of this table, grab him by his designer-label jacket and scream in his face. Why her? Why Jez? And why, as I sit here, staring at him, fighting desperately not to just fall apart because I'm shaking so hard, do I feel his hands touching me the way my dream says they touched my sister? My hair is pinned up, but I *feel the caress as he bares the back of my neck. The strength of his arms pull me back on his lap, holding me against his strong chest. Needles in the glove he wears on his other hand prick and scrape as his fingers steal in between my thighs. There's pleasure in his touch, pain of the pinpricks, and the most unbearable wanting in the flick of his tongue against my skin right before he covers the vein on the side of my neck in a suckling kiss...*

My heart thumps against my breastbone, startling me out of my dream-memories and back into the here and now.

"Aleron," he says, his hand still outthrust and waiting for mine. "Whom, may I ask, do I have the pleasure of conversing with?"

I confess, I have no idea what to do now. From the moment I had that first awful dream, I feel as if I've been running on instinct, grief, and very little sleep. I know his face. I now know his name. The man who killed my sister sits right across this table from me in a crowded nightclub that reeks of conflicting perfumes, sex, sweat and booze, and I can't prove a God damn thing.

A part of me wonders if I ever really thought I'd find him, much less the first time I gained access to this club. I have nothing prepared. He's asking my name, and the only thing I can think to say is, "You know who I am."

I don't take his hand, I don't want to touch any part of him. He notices and yet he's not offended. If anything, his amusement grows and he stands. Leaning over the table, giving me all the time in the world to yank away if I truly want to, he takes my hand anyway. Raising it to his lips, his eyes as black as a shark's, he kisses the backs of my fingers. My hand doesn't crawl the way it should. Instead, my fingers tingle where his lips have been.

He sits back down, licking his lips as if he can taste me on them, and I can tell he likes the flavor.

"I don't, actually," he corrects with a smile. "But I do know who you are not. My Jezebel has been buried for weeks now. I know, I visited her in the morgue, and I know the location of her grave."

My anger almost escapes my iron-clad will to suppress it. I'm shaking so hard I can't breathe. "You lying bastard."

The words almost choke me, my throat is so tight with anger and a rising swell of tears. I blink furiously to keep them back. I absolutely refuse to let him see me cry.

"True." His smile softens, but only just a little. "On both counts, although my mother did deny it. However, I *did* go to the morgue, and I *do* know where she is buried. And," he picks up his drink as if to salute her, "I know *you* are not her. Though I do believe everyone in this room thinks otherwise."

I couldn't care less about anyone else in this room. "Jez was my sister."

"Your twin," he adds, and it's all I can do not to slap the smirk from his face. "Yes, the likeness is flawless, but still, you are not her. You could give me your name, if you like. Or would you prefer I give you a new one?"

"As if I would answer." I can't imagine the circumstance in which that would happen.

His smile broadens. "Would you care to make a wager on it?"

"Would you care to make a wager?" he whispers in Jez's ear...

My head spins. For a moment, the nightclub recedes into blackness, and all I can hear is him *murmuring those words into Jez's ear, soft as a lover. All I see is the glide of his gloved fingers following the curve of my sister's mons down between her legs. Chains clink—her hands are bound in manacles high above her head, pulling her taut onto her tiptoes. A bar between her ankles prevents her legs from snapping shut, and yet, her gasp as the tiny spikes embedded in his gloves prick and scrape her most sensitive folds sounds wanton, not agonized...*

I flinch as the room snaps back into the loud and crowded present. A dull thump of unwelcome arousal pulses once between my tightly pressed legs. I refuse to let myself feel that of all sensations. Fine. Let him know who I am.

"Merris," I say.

Let him know exactly who's coming for him. For what he's done.

"Merris." He samples the flavor of my name the way he'd sampled the taste of my skin, seeming to find it to his liking. "I am very sorry for your loss."

Liar. He says those comforting words without the slightest hint of sympathy. I think he must be incapable of it. His eyes look dead.

Sliding closer, he edges around to my side of the booth, lowering both his voice and his head as he inquires, "Just allow me to say, darling Merris—"

I want to kill him.

"—although I know you're not likely to believe me—"

Not a word that comes out of his murderer's mouth.

"—I did not kill your sister." His eyes stay locked on mine, completely untouched by the warmth of his smile. "All those angry little accusations I see lurking inside you. Did I know your sister? Yes, I did. Did I play with her? Oh, absolutely. Did I speak with her the night she died? Yes. Do you want to know what I did? What she said? What happened to her as far as I know it—the truth, the whole truth, and nothing but, so help us all?" His mocking smile dims. For the first time I think I glimpse a touch of sincerity as he says again, "I did not kill your sister. But if it's answers that bring you to me, then ask your questions. Whatever they are, I will tell you what I know."

I know better than to trust a thing he says. The promise of a liar is worthless. And yet, in the shadows of the night-club, to my foolish tear-filled eyes, he seems so sincere. And suddenly, I feel nothing but tired.

Blame it on the grief, the alcohol I hadn't yet started

23

drinking but probably would before the night was out. Certainly, blame it on my lack of sleep, but I shake my head, and then I agree.

"Fine," I say, determined—at least for a while—to believe this man, Aleron.

It's not the first mistake I've made tonight.

And it won't be my last.

 *leron*

SHE'S NOT GOING to believe a word I say, but that's all right. I have been many things over the course of my very long life. Right now, it suits me to be a man of my word.

What can it hurt? She has tickled my fancy with her intrigue, but while I do believe I've now solved the puzzle of her, I feel oddly disinclined to end the game quite yet. I might still get a supper out of this. Besides, while I am not to blame for Jez's death, a part of me does wonder had I forced her surly, pouting, diminutive self into my car that night, would she still be alive? But I did not force her. I left her where she was, an adult capable of making her own bad decisions. Unfortunately, like most cities, Tucson is place of predators. After I left her, someone more dangerous came along.

That was not my fault.

I refuse to scourge myself over the death of a being who was doomed to die anyway, practically from the moment it drew its first squalling breath. Jez was always fated to die.

So too is her lovely, angry sister.

Tender-hearted fool I am not, but for just a moment, I find myself feeling for her. It's an awkward, uncomfortable thing. I haven't felt for anyone in ages. This must be one of those melancholy moments I so often hear about from my contemporaries. The ones in which they remember the loss of those they once loved. Family members, sweethearts, lovers, children if they had any before they were sired into this new life. Death after death. Year after heartless year, because that is the fate of mortals and immortals alike. They drop like flies into the abyss of memory, and we watch them go until we at last become immune to the sting.

For the sake of my stinging emotions, I decide to humor the girl. I know very little that can help her, but she has tracked her angry way to my table and for that, perhaps, she deserves some answers. And I... well, I'm going to give them to her because it amuses me. But after my cat and mouse is done and I've shared with her what little I know, I'll wipe her mind. I won't steal her memories of her sister or the pain of her loss, but I will send little Merris home. I no longer remember what the appropriate length of grieving time for mortals should be, but the last thing the vampires of Club Toxic need is an angry human on a mission, poking around our hunting ground.

That's how vampire and witch hunts get started. And frankly, they still sell vampire hunting kits on eBay.

Pushing her drink away with a shaking hand, she folds her arms on the table and leans toward me. I see a storm full of challenge churning in the soft gray of her eyes. The flesh of her breasts plump above the low cut of her clubbing dress too. They are small, a proper handful. I wouldn't mind seeing more of them.

"The whole truth?" she echoes.

"So help me God," I assure her. Even with these few inches of empty air between us, I feel the seductive heat emanating from her living body. I hear the steady beat of her pulse too. The minute leap of pale skin at the side of her neck shows me exactly where the artery lies. I can almost taste the sweetness of it.

"Why her?" She tries so hard to swallow back her anger so her voice doesn't quaver as she asks the first question. "What made you choose her?"

I know what she's really asking. Of all the people in the world, why did I kill her twin?

Except I didn't. A man can only proclaim his innocence for so long before he starts to sound guilty, even to himself.

I smile and choose instead to deliberately misunderstand.

"I chose Jez," I muse, for the first time in centuries actually attempting to dissect my own hunting process for the elusive 'why'. Why does one darling deer seem tastier than another? I land on the answer, and although I know it won't please her, I give it to her anyway. "Because she fell quite drunkenly into my lap." And why not just say it?

27

After all, I did promise her the truth. And since I do plan to strip it from her mind afterward, why not—as they say—bare all? "I was too hungry at the time to say no, and she was every bit my preference."

"Helpless?" Merris guessed, her gray eyes flaming with indignation.

"Lovely," I reply. "A bit shorter than I like, but curved in all the right places and, even more intoxicating, she was curious. She made me an offer I chose not to refuse."

"She made you an offer." Ah. I've pricked my puzzle's curiosity. "What offer?"

"Anything I wanted for nothing more than the cost of a drink."

She fights not to flinch, but I know that struck a nerve. She doesn't want to believe her sister would be that foolish, but I was hardly the first Jez had made such an offer to, and it seems we both know it.

"Liar," she says again, but she's trembling.

"Frequently," I agree. "But not about this. I've promised you the truth, and I'm content to give it. Our darling Jez did so like to party. She was an adventurous soul. Adventurous souls don't often think about the consequences they provoke, especially when a dance or a kiss is all a pretty girl thinks she has to pay to keep the party going with one more drink in her hand. So, I bought her a drink—a strawberry vodka lemonade. She was rather fond of them."

She's fighting to hold my stare. "And you put something in it."

My puzzle pricks my curiosity again. "No, why would I? She'd already promised me anything, and you and I

28

both know Jez was fantastically, shall we say, enthusiastic about keeping such promises." Folding my arms on the table, I lean towards her again. "Her only mistake that night—"

"The night you killed her," she accused.

"No, no, no." I brush that aside with a wave of one hand. "None of this happened the night she died, this was weeks earlier. You asked why I chose her. I chose her because I was bored, and hungry, and she fell into my lap. At which point, she promptly wrapped an arm about my neck and nibbled my ear. Being something of an ear nibbler myself, it got my attention. That is why I chose her."

The pulse at the base of Merris's neck jumps, and for just a moment, her eyes go strange. Unfocused. Her breath catches and beneath the thin cloth of her little black dress, the tips of her nipples bead up like pebbles. I don't often notice such things. Nipples are pretty, but after almost nine hundred years, I've seen my share. These days, when I gaze lovingly upon a human body, all I see are artery pathways. I've already mapped Merris's out—neck, inner thigh, clitoris.

I'll bet she has a tasty clit.

I can all but taste the swollen nub growing beneath the lash of my attentive tongue and it's all I can do not to salivate.

"My sister was not a prostitute," she breathes, blinking back the sheen of angry tears.

There it is again. That awkward, sympathetic feeling rising in my chest. The one that makes me want to spare her the additional hurt. I don't. She wants to know, so I'll tell her. When it's over, though, I'll be kind. I'll take away the pain and fill her head with happy thoughts instead, sending her back out into the world without a trace of suspicion left to unquiet her restless soul.

"We're all prostitutes," I gently correct. "Look at me. I paid your sister a drink for what she gave me. Look at you," I press, even more gently. "What would you not pay right here, right now, to find out what that was?"

She glares at me, her brow creased with equal measures hate and despair. She looks away, but almost as fast, her gaze locks once more on mine with a renewed glint of determination rolling in the stormy depths. "What do you want?"

I pretend to think about it. "Offer me what she did, and I'll not just tell you what happened, I'll show you."

Her eyes flash. "I am not a prostitute either."

I tsk. "I didn't sleep with your sister any more than I killed her." And then, just in case she wanted to squabble over semantics, added, "I didn't fuck her either."

Her pretty cheeks pinken. I don't think she wants to know, and yet she can't seem to stop herself. "What did she give you?"

"An hour of her time." The hunter in me cues in on every subtle nuance of her wavering expression as I add, "In which, she gave me anything I asked of her."

Her eyes narrowed. "But not sex?"

"What we shared was far more intimate, I promise you." I smile. "Are you intrigued?"

"Not even close."

"Naughty girl," I chide. "Be careful I don't take you over my knee for lying. You are absolutely intrigued."

My little puzzle girl likes mystery every bit as much as I do. She's practically squirming in her seat, trying to unravel all the hidden things I'm not saying. Leaning even closer, I lower my voice as much as the loud thumping music will allow and sweeten the pot. "Everything she gave me, she gave right here in this building. Darling, we'll barely have to leave the room."

Shoving away from the table, she leans back in her seat, probably because it's the only escape she can take without actually running away. She glares at me. "She wasn't found in this building."

Oh, we are stubbornly one-track-minded when we want to be.

"Merris," I say with exaggerated patience. "I already told you. I'm not talking about the night she died. I'm talking about the night we met. If you want to know what happened the night she died, I'll happily tell you that too, but you won't understand the latter event if you don't understand the first. Yes or no, my darling would-be prostitute, albeit of the infinitely more fascinating intellectual variety. How badly do you want to know the answers to your questions?"

She really is innocent. She has no idea how easy it is to read all the thoughts flitting across her expressive, young face. She doesn't believe or trust me, but she wants to. She wants to find out more than anything, but she's afraid of what she'll learn.

"We don't leave this building?" she asks.

She thinks the crowd in Club Toxic will keep her safe. She has no idea how many vampires have become aware of her since she walked into this room.

"Not so much as a step out the front door," I reply, and I don't even have to soothe my conscience because that is not a lie. The Dungeon can't be accessed from the street or the alleyway. It lies in the basement, and like a lamb to the proverbial slaughter, she's going to follow me right to it.

∾

Merris

I'M NOT RUNNING AWAY from him. I'm going to the damn bathroom.

That's what I tell myself as I walk as slowly as I possibly can, crossing the dark lounge floor, feeling eyes on me every step of the way.

"Girl, someone said you were dead," one of the wait-resses hisses as I stalk by her, but I don't stay to talk. I duck my head, feeling sick to my stomach. Barely making it to the bathroom, I shove open the door and knock into a woman coming out.

"Hey!" she squawks, but I don't stop.

Of the three bathroom stalls, only one isn't occupied, and no sooner am I inside with the door slammed and locked behind me, then does my rolling stomach rebel. I barely get positioned in time, but nothing comes out. It's just dry heaving that breaks down after the second gasp until I hang my head and sob.

Someone hesitantly knocks on the stall door.

"I'm fine," I snap. Grabbing wads of tissue on which to

wipe my mouth and eyes, in as calm a voice as I'm able, I try again. "I just had too much to drink."

Whoever it is, after a half-second's pause, they go away. The sounds of the busy club outside this room get louder with the opening of the door, then they grow muffled again as the door drifts shut. Everything in the bathroom is quiet now. All I can hear is me—my ragged breathing, my pathetic sniffling, the battering of my pulse in my head, at war with the pulse of the bass in the club speakers.

What am I doing here?

What am I trying to accomplish?

I ought to leave right now and… and, what? Go tell the cops I found the owner of the face that haunts my dreams? That every night I see the way he gropes and touches my dead sister, and based on *that* evidence, what do I expect them to do? Because it's far more likely to involve me in a psych-ward over him in a jail cell.

Pushing myself up off the floor, I lean back against the door and try to stop shaking. What am I doing here? If I really do think this man is responsible for Jez—and I do, I have to; my dreams are often confusing but they've never lied to me before—then what good will come from anything he tells me?

The details of what she gave him are so stark in my mind. I know he strips her naked. I know he chains her up, spreads her legs, lets his hand wander down between her legs in ways no one wants to see anyone be with their sister.

What good will come of following this man and hearing from his lips exactly what he did to her?

My hands shaking, I blow my nose one last time, throw the tissue in the toilet and then reach into my purse and turn my cellphone on. I've got a voice-recording app on here that lasts upwards of an hour. It's useless out there where the music is so loud, but if I can get him to take me somewhere quieter, and I can get him to admit something worth taking to the police, then maybe, just maybe, I can put my sister's killer behind bars.

It's not like he can kill me in the middle of this crowded nightclub. So long as I don't leave with him, I know I'll be fine. I just have to keep it together long enough to get something damning out of him. I'll go straight to the police afterward. Finally, they'll have no choice but to do their jobs.

My sister wasn't a whore.

Neither am I, but Aleron is right. There's nothing I wouldn't do to catch his confession on a digital soundbite file.

Absolutely nothing.

Does that include fucking my sister's killer? I steel myself for the possibility, tuck the phone down into an outside pocket of my purse where I hope it might have a better chance to pick up our conversation unnoticed, and I pray I won't have to. But 'nothing' does mean nothing, and the weirdest thing happens in the pit of my belly at the thought of him touching me the way I keep seeing in my mind. I can tell myself it's because just the thought of it makes me sick, but the truth is this doesn't feel like revulsion.

Scrubbing my sweaty palms against my skirt-clad thighs, I walk back out of the bathroom.

Aleron is exactly where I left him, head tilted to one side, the corner of his devilish mouth curling as he watches me cross the floor back to him. I'm almost to him before he slides out of the booth and stands. He's taller than I am, broader in the shoulders, and he looks far more powerful now that he's on his feet than while he was sitting. His is an air of wealth, power, calm masculinity, and God... that smile.

My nipples react against my will. And that's even before he holds out an arm as if to draw me in under his wing. I don't get that close, but when he gestures for me to precede him, the touch of his hand settles light on my back, between my shoulder blades. He guides without words and I go where he tells me, the shortest route out between the crush of people crowding the tables in the lounge, around the periphery of the dance floor. I don't realize he's taking me to the coat closet until we draw abreast of the security guards and the subtle nudge of his hand changes my direction.

The guards look at us, but they make no move to stop him. Or me.

"I don't have a coat," I say, trying to hide my nervousness. I don't know why we'd need it anyway. He already said we weren't leaving the club.

I don't even see what he touches, but suddenly a section of what I thought was solid wall has opened into blackness, revealing stairs that lead down.

That blackness stops me. My heart slams once against my chest wall and then I feel nothing, just the subtle brush of an air-conditioned breeze wafting up the staircase as he waits to see if I'll... what, run screaming? I want to.

Staring down into that darkness, I can't imagine what awaits me at the bottom.

"You didn't take her down here," I say, hating the quiver of fear I can't hide in my voice.

"I did," he countered, and I can hear both the amusement and the challenge in his as he adds, "She came most willingly... repeatedly, even, although I'm generally not one to boast."

As if my brain needs the reminder. The visions haven't been far from my thoughts from the moment I came here tonight. I move forward, resting a hand for balance on the cool wall as I step down into the shadows of the stairwell. The light from above bleeds down into inky nothingness, from which I just barely detect... muffled sounds. Whimpers. Moans. The distant clap of skin striking skin, not sharp or loud, but softly.

Sex?

"Don't be afraid," he coaxes from behind me. "I promise, my darling Merris, nothing down there will hurt you."

"Except you?" I challenge. My response makes him laugh, a low throaty chuckle that both shivers me and makes my nipples pebble harder.

"I'm not down there yet."

And here I'd have thought it smarter to assure me he wouldn't hurt me. Nervous as I am, I don't realize I've said that out loud until Aleron laughs again.

"Oh, but I promised I wouldn't lie. Nothing but the truth," he reminds. "However, if it makes you feel better, I promise nothing I do will prevent you from walking back out of here when we are done, your questions all answered to the best of my knowledge, and I won't lay one hand on you until you ask me to."

I snap around to stare at him, eyes narrowing at the way he's watching me. A predator herding me down into the dark.

What would you pay...

For my sister? I face the bottom of the steps again and, steeling myself against the black, down I go.

The narrow high heels of my shoes descending the steps send echoes back up through the stairwell. The light from above doesn't want to follow us down. With every step, I am losing my ability to see. Already this flight of stairs seems far longer than any normal flight should be. How far I am from the bottom, I don't know, but I stop when he taps my shoulder.

"I'm going to reach past you," he cautions.

The bare flesh all up and down my arms prickle, sending shivers across the back of my neck a half second before I feel the brush of his coat. A latch clicks and suddenly the blackness is broken by the opening of a door. The light down here is dim, but at least there is light, and God help me, does it ever set a mood.

I have never been in such a place before, but I know automatically exactly what this is. The basement of Club Toxic is a dungeon. Not as in castle or prison, but as in BDSM and... yes, okay, prison. The music here is darker, deeper, rhythmic bass thumpings that make my heart beat along in nervous time. The light strips along the ceiling cast red-bulb illumination on the strangest of furniture. A giant wooden X, a variety of padded benches, a steel cage in one corner, and black-painted walls studded with massive steel rings from which one woman is already tied.

Wrists bound, she is stripped as naked as Jez in my dreams. Facing the wall, she grips the ring while the equally naked man behinds her slashes at her back, again and again, with a multi-tailed flogger. The sound of it striking her makes me jump. Her answering moan, however, goes straight through me, igniting dull pulses of fire in key places that I am not at all comfortable feeling. My breasts grow heavy as my breath catches in my throat. My muscles tighten, pussy clenching sharply even as heat flows molten all the way down to dampen the crotch of my panties.

Before I can stop myself, I move closer and almost walk right into that man's swinging flogger.

Aleron catches my arm, pulling me back before I'm caught by those slapping tips, but I feel the rush of air as they fly harmlessly past me. Flinching another step back, I bump into Aleron even as the man, catching my retreat from the corner of his eye, glances back at us. He checks his distance automatically, his shadowed gaze moving over me even as he frowns.

"Your pardon," Aleron says, anything but apologetic. When he pulls, I follow and we move away. "Dimitri likes to play by the door," he tells me, his voice low against my ear. "He enjoys catching the unwary on a backswing when they least expect it."

Dimitri and his naked woman aren't our only company in this place, though. Passing a doorway, I hear the unmistakable sound of vigorous sex—the wet slapping, the moaning, the hungry suckling of a mouth breaking suction with skin to the muffled accompaniment of a mewl of disappointment. And in the very back, on a raised dais under the glow of another strip of red lights, a man is chained to a ceiling hoist, pulled high up onto tiptoes while a woman kneels, breasts bared, her dress a puddle of silver sequins and white cloth around her waist. Her mouth attentively works his high-standing cock. She wears a collar, just like the workers upstairs, and behind the man she's working on, a taller man moves into position at his back. Taking hold of the chained man's throat, he adjusts himself with his other hand and before my astonished eyes, tension ripples the chained man's body as he's invaded from behind.

Pain and pleasure warble his long groan as the taller man begins to pump. He is not gentle. The hoist clinks, jostling with each hard thrust, and the woman's actions escalate to match. As if on cue, the tall man and woman both bite and the chained man stiffens with a shout. His whole body shakes in orgasm, and I can't look away. Not even when Aleron takes my arm, drawing me stumbling through a velvet curtain into a very dark, semi-private alcove.

I fall back against the wall as soon as I'm inside, my heart battering wildly, my own ragged breaths suffocating me, so appalled and alarmed and, God, even aroused, that I can barely recognize myself.

"What is this?" I demand, and yet the very warble of my voice is at once strangled and lustful and incredulous. "No way did my sister come down here with you!"

Aleron does not move closer, but never have I been more aware of a man in my life.

"She did," he states, and I know he's not lying. Not because he confirms his dubious promise to tell me only the truth, but because I *can see it. The nakedness of a body exactly like mine, drawn up by the manacles on her wrist, her bare pale breasts filling up Aleron's kneading hands, as they squeeze, pluck and lightly tweak to make the budding nipples stand for him. Ache for him.*

Unlike the man out there, he's fully clothed, the dark of his expensive jacket contrasting sharply with the white of her skin as he pulls on his gloves. They rake me from breasts to belly and hips to thighs, the needle-studded leather dragging across my skin as if it were actually happening to me.

I shake my head, feeling the slip of those imaginary fingers stealing in between my wildly trembling thighs as the real Aleron slips a single step closer. His actual hand, bare, void of the prickling spikes scraping my clit in my mind, braces on the wall beside my head.

"Buy me a drink, she asked me," Aleron says, soft as a lover. I can smell the tequila on the breath that kisses my cheek. I can smell the spice of his cologne. It's faint, neither cloying nor overpowering. It plays with my senses every bit as wildly as the visions in my head. I can smell his cologne there too. It's the same dizzying formula of spices. He's wearing the same coat too.

The gloves... My vision tells me where they are, tucked together in a neat fold inside an inner jacket pocket.

"So, I did. Strawberry vodka lemonade, she loved them."

She did, too. I've never understood why. The damn things taste horrible to me. A watery suffocation of tears

40

rise up in the back of my throat. My eyes pick the stupidest things to cry over.

"I held it out to her," Aleron gently says, and in the dark of this falsely private room, I can find nothing in his expression that says he's lying. "I said, *what will you do for it?* Her reply was open flirtation. *What do you want me to do?*"

In my mind I can hear him saying, *Anything is a broad promise,* followed by Jez's throaty laugh. *Don't worry about me. I'm a big girl. I know what I'm doing.*

"*Anything* is what she assured me," Aleron says. "So, I lay the drink upon the table and said that she may have it, plus anything else she wanted for the duration of the night for the price of one hour of her time in which she did whatever I asked. I played with her, my darling Merris, and then I let her go. She was here perhaps three or four hours afterward, then she went home. Quite intoxicated, but none the worse for all the yummy things I did to her."

"You drugged her," I accuse, "and you took advantage of her."

His jaw clenches and for the first time, a nuance of his amusement dies. A vague shade of anger takes its place. "I did not," he replies, dangerously soft. "I have no need of drugs, and my cock did not leave my trousers the entire time I played with her. That was not what I wanted her for."

"You fucked her," I insist.

Again, he keeps his smile, but the aura of his amusement diminishes and anger rises a notch higher. He keeps a tight rein on it, though. Swallowing it back, no hint of the emotion shows in his voice as he counters, "Would you like a play by play of exactly what I did?"

My pussy clenches wildly. No, I do not. But I do want to know. I have to know. I need proof and to fill in the holes my visions tease me with.

Mine are the best of intentions.

What is it they say about the road to hell?

$\mathcal{M}$*erris*

"You'll show me," I specify, not moving. "You'll tell me exactly what you did."

"You give me deed for deed, I'll pay you word by word," he promises. "If we're going to do it, however, we need to get started. What I want takes time, the employees will start shooing people out soon, and all private parties must be completed by 4:00 a.m."

"And I just walk out of here when we're done?"

"Exactly as she did, yes."

"Unharmed?"

"Mm." His is an alluring smile, one full of challenge, secrets and, reluctant though I am to admit it, seduction. It pulls at me. "More or less."

I don't trust him. I can't afford to, but not knowing is eating me alive. When he holds out his hand, I take it, but his request for consent is little more than symbolic, and my granting of it leaves me shaking. He only draws me two steps from the wall before allowing my hand to drop. Hugging my arms, I watch as he takes off his coat. His shoulders seem so much broader without it. His shirt is tailor-made, the bright whiteness of it a ghostly pallor that cuts the shadows in this dimly lit place.

That he can see so much better in the dark is obvious. I can't even see where he drew that chair from. I can barely make out the black lines of it as he sets it in the middle of our semi-private room and sits, unbuttoning and rolling up his shirt cuffs to his elbows.

Unmoving, I watch him. The red of the ceiling lights is definitely creating a mood in here too. I blame them for what's happening to me—the tightening in my belly, the tensing of my thighs growing tighter while I watch turn after neat turn of his shirt sleeves reveal inch after hard, muscular inch of his forearms. He is far more muscular than any man that slender should be. Who is this guy? Model… movie star… body builder… fucking American Ninja Warrior? I've no idea, but what he does shouldn't be as important as what he has done. He killed my sister. I hold on to that belief with both hands. My visions have never been wrong before, but while they never actually showed me her moment of death, I know he was with her. I *know* it.

He beckons me to him with a crook of his finger.

I stare at him, sitting in that chair. If he's expecting a lap dance, he's shit out of luck. They tried to teach me to jitterbug in the sixth grade for a school play once. They ended up putting me with the band on a triangle instead.

I'm not sexy. I'm not graceful. I barely even qualify as a girl, and it's all I can do just to walk straight in these heels.

"Come," he coaxes, then adds the one thing he knows I can't make myself refuse. "You want to know, don't you?"

I go to him, but my body is so tense and I can't stop myself from shaking. A few steps is all I manage, but it's enough to bring me within his reach. My knee is just inches from his. I try hard not to stare at his lap or the paleness of his hands in the dark of this room, or, God help me, the bulge in the crotch of his pants not far from where his hand now rests upon his thigh.

"I told her to bend across my knee," he says, his shadowy eyes watching me. "She laughed, but that was the price of my drink. She called me kinky"—a quick twist of a smile flashes pale teeth, but it's there and gone again just as quickly—"but she did it. Upstairs. In the middle of the lounge, surrounded by people laughing, talking, drinking... flirting every bit as much as we were. I think I intrigued her, but then, as I already said, Jez was an adventurous soul."

She was, too. I swallow hard when he pats his thigh. I look at it, and then at him, and slowly it dawns on me what he expects of me. It's not a lap dance.

"You want to spank me?" I saw no visions of him doing anything like that to Jez.

"You do for me what she did, and I will tell you what I know."

That was the deal, he's right. But somewhere along the way, it took a decidedly kinky turn.

I feel absolutely ridiculous as I edge in on his right, eyeing his hands and his lap and feeling my bottom inexplicably crawling. It's the strangest sensation—prickly with something I can only liken to anticipation, although that has to be wrong. It has to be. Every bit as wrong as the flood of wet heat that spills down through my secret folds as I reluctantly lower myself into place. He helps guide me down over thighs that are so much harder beneath my stomach and my hand than I expected. This is so alien to me. I cup his knee, but I don't know how or where to touch him.

He doesn't have that same problem with me. Without a word, he reaches under the skirt of my short dress. His hand is surprisingly cool when he cups the inside of my thigh. His arm wraps my waist and in a short, lift-pull motion, he heaves me further over his lap. My feet leave the floor, but only my quick-bracing slap with both hands keeps my nose from bumping into it on the other side.

This is insane.

His arm stays around my waist, holding me in place. His other hand raises my skirt all the way up to my hips, baring the fabric of my underwear.

They weren't my sexiest pair. Why would they be? I hadn't come to the club tonight planning to show my butt to anyone and certainly not Aleron.

"Relax," he soothes, letting his fingers trace a wandering pattern over my vulnerably exposed backside.

That's easy for him to say. He's not the one letting a killer eyeball his powder-blue boyshorts. For the first time all night, I'm grateful the boxers I normally like messed with the lines of the dress.

"This is interesting," he says, one finger lightly tracing along the elastic leg seam of my shorts. "If I hadn't already known you weren't your twin, this would have told me. I never saw your sister in anything but a thong."

He raised his hand and I braced to be struck. My second surprise comes a half second later, when his fingers tap lightly down in a gentle pat upon the center of my left buttock. Pulling my skirt down, he promptly draws me up to sit upon his knee.

"I spanked her upstairs," he says. "She was not a fan, but she was delightfully determined to withstand whatever I chose to do and that appealed to me. So, I set her bottom on fire and only when I was sure I had her right on the edge of crying out her safeword, did I stop."

My visions had shown me none of that. Maybe I should be glad, because as it was, my imagination is having no trouble at all conjuring how that might have played out. Only, it isn't my sister I can see squirming and writhing under the steady assault of his open palm. It's me, my bottom that he paints red one sharp slap at a time until I can't make myself stay quiet or hold still.

My breasts ache. My nipples swell with such need, that it's all I can do to keep the huskiness of my arousal from telling in my voice. "What do you mean, *safeword*?"

"A safeword is any chosen word that you can use at any time, and I will immediately stop what I am doing."

I scoff, hardly able to imagine it. He had to think me stupid.

There his eyes go again, sparking with amusement and issuing challenges. "Would you like one?"

As if he'd honor it.

I already know he won't. Because, of course he won't.

That was beyond ridiculous. Whoever heard of a word stopping a killer? It's insane!

Isn't it?

"Pick one," he dares me. "Something unusual. Something you wouldn't ordinarily cry out in, say, the throes of an orgasm."

Heat burns up through my belly and into my face. I try to get up off his knee, to put at least a few inches of distance between us again. Ashamed though I am to admit it, I can imagine only too well how it might feel to have him bring me to orgasm.

I don't like this. I can't think when I'm sitting in his lap, feeling his chest against my side and his arm around my waist with the light press of his relaxed hand cupping my hip. Instead of moving, however, I surprise myself by saying, "Fine. Um…" I try to think of a word, but I'm not very good at these sorts of games. "Rumpelstiltskin."

He's trying not to laugh at me. "Rumpelstiltskin," he agrees with a nod. "This is how it works. If at any point you find yourself unable to continue while I do to you what I did to her, use that word."

"And you'll stop." I don't know if I can believe it when he nods, but I grudgingly agree. "All right."

"I finish spanking her and tell her to stand." Aleron looks at me expectantly.

It takes a minute for me to figure out that he's waiting for me to comply. I'm only too happy to get off his lap.

"I tell her to remove her panties." Leaning back in his chair, he folds his strong arms and waits.

I'd love to say I can't imagine Jez putting on a panty strip-show for anyone in the middle of a nightclub, but unfortunately, I can. Reaching under my skirt, I shuck my underwear with little patience for mind games. If he thinks I'm going to hand them over as some kind of trophy of the night, he's out of his mind.

"She hands them to me," he says, lazily rolling out his hand, palm up, and waits again.

Asshole.

I slap my underwear into his palm and watch as he drops them on the floor beside his chair. I am insanely more bothered by them lying there than I'd have been had he stuffed them in his pocket. A tiny spot between my shoulder blades itches with my growing discomfort, and yet there's this horrible, anticipatory tingling in my breasts, my belly... my hands that longs for me to leap at him, snatch my underwear up off the floor and quickly tuck them out of sight. I feel so scandalously embarrassed not to be wearing them right now, in front of him, while all the while he knows all he had to do to get me out of them had been a subtle word on his part.

And the lack of a certain word on mine.

"I told her to sit upon my knee."

My jaw hurts from the force with which I clench my teeth. Coming to him, I lower myself as primly as possible onto his lap.

"She straddled me, actually." He smiles as he corrects me. "I didn't ask her to. She did that all on her own."

Snapping up off him, I scrub my sweaty palms down the front of my skirt. My legs are shaking too hard to walk away. My heart feels both caged and wild, but I've come too far to just leave, especially over something as reluctantly titillating as being made to straddle his thighs.

My dress skirt is too tight. I have to hike it up to the tops of my thighs in order to straddle him. His shoulder is solid and strong, and cool to the touch when I settled my hand upon him for balance and gingerly lower myself to sit.

He doesn't touch me with his hands. He doesn't have to. I feel positively molested by all the places of him that inadvertently brush against me. With every breath, my breasts caress his chest. I can't feel the beating of his heart beneath the barrier of both our clothes, but I feel mine and it's savage. Pounding so hard. So hot. Making me burn in a fire that feels like more than embarrassment. It may center in my chest, but it doesn't stay there. Already the heat is wending its way through me, filling my womb, spilling down into my empty sex until the trickling moisture weeps from me. I can still feel the phantom pat he swatted me with, right before he stole my panties. My bottom cheek is pulsing. Like the heat inside me, it throbs until this dull aching is all I feel.

And I don't want to. God, how I don't want to. Not for this man.

"By this time, we were down here," Aleron says. Watching my reaction closely, he raises a hand to my cheek to brush a stray wisp of hair from my eyes with the back of his finger. "I tell her to turn around. I want her back to my chest, and we shall play a game."

"What kind of game?" My voice trembles as badly as the rest of me. I sound breathless, and he can't help but hear it.

He smiles again, that lazy smile that says nothing, as he simply waits until I obey him.

My legs shake, but up I stand. There are a thousand reasons why I should not turn my back to him, but this is a public place, I remind myself. There are people down here. He wouldn't dare hurt me where he can so easily be caught.

Backing up, I lower myself again to straddle his lap, this time facing away from him. His muscular thighs beneath me are breathtakingly hard. I lean back slowly until I am pressed against his chest. I'm afraid I'll feel it, but there is no bulging erection pushing up against my ass. I am as oddly disappointed as I'm relieved.

"Our game will be simple," Aleron says. "Using nothing but my hands, I am going to make you come. Using nothing but your will, you are going to resist me. If you succeed, you will have done better than your sister. If I succeed, then I get a prize."

"What prize?" I doubt I need to ask. I'm almost certain I know exactly what form his 'prize' will take.

"A kiss," he says simply, surprising me. "Right here." His cool lips press briefly to the side of my neck where he can't help but feel the pulsing thump of my wanton heart fluttering at his touch.

"That's it?" I ask, highly doubtful. "You kissed my sister?"

"She lost the game in less than eleven minutes."

I crane my head to stare at him.

"Did I fail to mention the time limit?" he asked, amused. "Bad Aleron. Yes, there's a time constraint. If I can't bring you to come within twenty, then first and foremost, no one can, and second, you win the game."

"What do I get if I win?"

"A complete lack of gratification. I understand it's quite maddening."

I frown. "I'm being serious."

He huffs a soft sigh over my lack of humor. "How about I stop all further attempts to draw this out, tell you everything I know, introduce you to everyone your sister played down here with, and send you on your happy way. Deal?"

"Who's going to keep the time?"

Holding out his right arm, he shows me his wristwatch. "Cunning invention. It even has an alarm."

"All right, all right," I grumble, almost rolling my eyes. He really is an asshole.

"Is that agreement?"

Dropping his arms, his hands come to rest on my thighs. It's a light touch, completely impersonal, except it feels anything but to me. He doesn't stroke or caress me, but I still feel the flutter of my pulse at how just a shift of his fingers could—and would, if I agree to this—have him touching other places.

If it gets me the answers I crave…

Shamefully, it's not answers I'm thinking about when I jerk my head in a consenting nod. It's the heat, and the throb, and the way my skin tingles all the way down into my nipples when he touches his lips to my neck.

"Twenty minutes," I say. Not one second more.

To be perfectly honest, I'm not at all sure I'll make it to eleven.

"Twenty minutes," he echoes in agreement, taking hold of my skirt and giving the form-fitting fabric a brisk tug, baring me front and back all the way to my waist. He is just as impersonal when he dips his hands into the neckline of my dress, tugging my sleeves down off my shoulders and scooping my breasts out into the open. My nipples are hard, tight little peaks that only tighten harder when his cool breath tickles my ear. "You don't mind if I wear gloves, do you?"

He takes them from the inner pocket of his coat, draped as it is over the back of his chair. It's a theatrical production, watching him slip his hands into the black leather.

"They're called vampire gloves."

I shiver as he turns his gloved hands over and what dim light there is catches on the pointed tips of the metal spikes protruding down the lengths of each finger.

"Don't be afraid," he soothes when I shiver as he brings his hand up to my face. "As you are about to discover, a little bite of pain"—the tip of one finger touches lightly behind my jaw at the lobe of my ear—"can make the pleasure"—he scrapes me, following the line and raising chills as he passes below my chin and around my neck—"so much sweeter."

His trailing finger wanders down my neck onto my chest at the same time I feel the spikes of his other gloved hand come to rest on the inside of my left thigh. Those fingers scrape lightly upward, following the inner slope of my thigh all the way to where every single one of my nerve endings is ready to riot.

That's when I know for certain.

I definitely won't make eleven minutes.

~

Aleron

SHE'S A PLEASANT ARMFUL, I'll give her that. Her breasts are just the right size, a comfortable fit in my palm as I lightly flick and scrape the buds of her nipples with the biting spikes of my gloves. Her body straddles mine as if she were made for me. The heat of her ass burning through my clothes has my body responding in ways it usually doesn't. Not for Jez. Not for anyone. Not for a very long time. I'm actually inspired to fuck. I feel unexpectedly young, my cock stirring beneath her, rising in search of her body heat.

It's the sweetness of her blood, I tell myself. The anticipation of the feed when I win. I can already smell it moving deliciously through her veins as I cup her pussy in my hand, releasing a wave of seductive pheromones that tantalize me. I can smell her arousal. That part isn't new, but feeling the tension in her body as she tries to fight me… oh, now that takes the pleasure to a whole new level.

I'm not a good man. I don't remember a point when I ever was. They say time tempers even the intemperate, and perhaps that's true. Because while these last few centuries I have been content to follow my brethren—walking, hunting, quietly existing among our chosen prey without humans being any the wiser for it—it only takes a semi-reluctant jerk of her hips grinding above my cock to remind me how good it is when the prey is not so willing.

She tries to turn her head away, as if she can't bear to watch, but almost as reluctantly, her gaze drifts back. She looks down at herself, each breath a tiny catch of disbelief at the sensations I wring from her.

I am so… gentle with her. Plucking her nipples, fighting the urge to pinch and tweak. Holding her in my arms as she writhes to the ever-increasing force of my patting hand as I spank her pretty pussy until the bite of the finger spikes aren't quite so gentle anymore, and she finally snaps her widely spread legs shut. It must prick even more to have my hand now captured between her squeezing thighs.

"Don't be naughty," I coax, low against the lobe of the ear I'd dearly love to bite. But I promised only my hands. Normally I love the challenge of my self-imposed restrictions, but not today. Today, every mewl of unexpected distress that falls from her lips rakes me every bit as sharply as if I have turned these gloves on myself. "Open for me."

That she doesn't want to is evident in the stop and start twitches of her legs as she slowly pries them apart.

I love her smell.

I am so… aroused. I can't remember the last time that has happened over something as simple as supper. I tell myself it's the puzzle of her, but perhaps it's simply the humping grind of her hot little ass wriggling about on my lap as I slip my spiked fingers up into her folds, parting her intimately, opening her up so I can freely enjoy her aroma.

She arches, throwing her head all the way back onto my shoulder, catching the side of my neck in her hot, desperate hand. Muffling her gasp behind tightly clenched lips when I find her clit.

I love it.

I scrape it.

The tiniest hint of fresh blood rises into the air and, going taut as a bowstring, she suddenly rolls her head, turning to bury her face in the side of my neck and biting. I feel the blunted nip of her human teeth. It's not hard, and there's no pain. But in that fragile miniscule of a half second, she turns me from predator to prey.

No one has ever done that before.

I feel… is that flash of white iciness… fear nipping at the side of my neck? Or is it pleasure unlike anything I have known in almost nine hundred years? I don't know, but my hand is in her hair, seizing a fistful of bobby pins and bun, yanking her head all the way back to rip her teeth from my flesh and bare the slender curve of her throat.

She gasps at the suddenness of it. Her body goes stiff and still, with her legs still widely spread and her thrusting nipples peaked for my touch. Her smell is exquisite, lust and sweet blood. Her muscles twitch, betraying just how closely I have her perched upon the edge of losing the game.

"I am the master," I tell her, laying my hand between her quivering legs. "I am the only one who bites."

One spank to punish. Despite my fondness for these gloves, I wish my hand were bare for that. I cup her femininity and heat—I wish my hand were bare for that too—and squeeze. She arches, shouting, grabbing on to my wrist and my neck.

I can't bear it.

Ripping the glove off with my teeth, I put two fingers to her mouth.

"Lick," I command.

She tries to turn away, but a shake of her captured hair turns her sweet and obedient again.

"Lick," I growl, and she does. The tip of her bedeviling tongue flicks out to leave its kiss of wetness upon the tips of my fingers.

"I am the master," I say again, reaching down between her legs. Her heat is the most exquisite I think I've ever felt. Her trembling as I touch her, skin to skin, is intoxicating.

"N-no," she moans, staring helpless up at the lights in the ceiling, but her clit is mine, and I make love to it with all the skill of a man who has devoted nine hundred years to learning the female body. For the last few centuries, it is a skill I have utilized by rote—without needing to think. Without needing to care.

What I do to little Merris in my arms is not done by habit. It does not feel like automated routine. It feels as fresh as the lingering sensation of her teeth still tingling my neck. It feels as hot as the burning of her sex as I sink my fingers into her. I feel every tightening spasm in her body. Her gasps, then squeaks, then despairing cries are the music that make my cold heart sing. She can't hold still. Her hips are rocking, riding my thrusting fingers with increasing franticness.

"No... no!" she cries, but 'no' is not our safeword, and I am having far too much fun to stop. "No!" she shouts, grabbing my wrist.

But 'yes' is the convulsion of the orgasm that rips through her body, bowing her upon my lap with a wrenching cry that echoes through the club dungeon. Her release is the sweetest victory I've yet held this close to my chest.

"I win," I whisper, but for the first time in a long time, I don't even bother to check my watch. I could care less about the game. I want her to come for me again. I want her to come while my cock is buried as deep into the beautiful heat of her as I can reach. I want to feel the wild beating of her heart as I press my naked chest to hers. I want to claim her—her mouth, her body—not just with mine, but also my teeth.

Sadly, none of that was promised to me.

The alarm on my watch beeps.

The tension in her body ebbs with the rolling spasms of her dying climax. She wilts, panting and whimpering in my arms. Normally, I'd have fed at the moment her orgasm hit her, but my lovely little puzzle had the temerity to bite me.

I hold her, rocking her, letting her come sweetly all the way back to herself before slowly tightening my arm around her waist. Nuzzling the side of her neck, I secure my grip on her hair, pulling her head to one side.

"What are you doing?" she asks in that sultry, hazy voice of a woman still lazying in the afterglow of her pleasure.

I lick her, savoring the taste of her skin, the feel of all that hot, sweet blood pulsing in the vein that lurks beneath my lips.

I let her feel the points of my teeth, and her body goes stiff.

Her breath catches. She no longer sounds like a well-fucked woman when she stammers, "Wh-what are you doing?"

"My kiss," I remind her. "Should I forget to tell you so later on, my darling Merris, I haven't had this much fun in years. Keep your legs open, please. I like the scent."

She closes them almost immediately, contrary little thing, and twists. She's not fighting me, not yet, but she is uncertain and wants to get up.

Given my preference, she would be naked on her knees before me every night for the rest of her life.

Sadly, that wasn't part of the game either.

"Naughty girl," I tell her fondly, and bite.

 *leron*

MERRIS STUMBLES, unsteady on her feet, but my hand at her elbow keeps her from falling as I guide her around to sit in the chair I vacated. The flush of the orgasms I gave her still pinken her skin. The rush of endorphins from my bite is probably still singing in all the places I fondled as I dined on her. I made her come twice more even as I drank from her. I could have drunk all night, but I'd rather not kill her. Honestly, I haven't killed in decades, but she was such an unexpected pleasure that I'll admit, I did find it hard to stop. I didn't want the contact between us to end.

Even now, her skirt remains gathered high around her waist and her panties are still on the floor. I should let her reclaim her dignity, but it seems such a waste to conceal the beauty of her behind clothes.

"What did you do to me?" she mumbles, reaching up

to touch her neck where the pinpricks of my bite still seep. The crimson drops are like jewels against the pallor of her skin.

I take her hand before she can touch and smear them. "I gave you a kiss," I tell her.

"You did the same to Jez?"

And of course, the conversation winds back to her sister. I shouldn't be surprised or half as annoyed by that as I am. "Yes, I did." Although I didn't make anywhere near as big a production out of letting Jez feel my teeth.

I hear the whisper of movement a spare second before a shadow darkens the crack around the velvet curtain that hangs over the open doorway to this semi-private play area. It's one of Club Toxic's household humans, the collar around her neck hiding the marks left behind by regular feedings. She has a tray in her hands, offerings of chocolate, juice or water, and bites of meat and cheese. Taking the tray, I send the girl off with instructions and a nod when at first, she only gives me a startled look. She does go, though, and for a few minutes, it's once more just Merris and I in the privacy of my favorite dining room.

"Here." I help her drink. Her hands shake slightly, either from her blood donation or the orgasms, I'm not sure. She eats cheese cubes and chocolate from my fingers, until gradually it comes back to her that we are erstwhile enemies. After that, she takes the offerings I give her, frowning at me as she eats.

"What did you do to me?" She tries again to touch her neck, but again, I take her hand.

"Don't touch," I admonish, giving the back of it a

playful slap before handing her another piece of chocolate. "Let me take care of that."

I bandage her, something the attendants here usually do. But my time with her is running out and I find myself content to horde what seconds I have left, keeping her all to myself rather than passing her into the care of someone else.

Besides, we made a bargain, she and I. I'm also content to keep my end of it.

"Give it a few days to heal, and you'll be fine."

"Did you break the skin?" She's very single-minded. This time when she reaches for her neck, I let her feel along the edges of the small square bandage. She pokes, testing for tenderness.

"Just a bit of blood play," I assure her. The standard answer. No sense scaring the buffalo before sending her back out into the herd. "But now you know everything I did to your sister. A few scintillating caresses in the shadows of this place, a nip on the neck, and then I fed her chocolates and sent her back upstairs where she had another drink before catching a cab for home. It was the only time I played with her. I never play with anyone twice."

I can see the spark of mistrust flare to angry life in her pretty eyes. "That's a lie."

Her insistence that I took her sister to bed, while perfectly in line with the air I like to portray, bothers me. "Is that what she told you?"

"She didn't have to. I—" She stops abruptly when the curtain draws aside and Leander, a vampire almost as old as I steps into the dark of our room.

He looks at the bandage on her neck, the tray in her lap, and then at me. I glimpse his annoyance that he wasn't being called to supper.

As if I'd share.

"You summoned?" he asks dryly. And then he recognizes her and his mask falls to open shock.

"This is Leander," I introduce. "Two nights after we played, Jez returned to the club and requested another 'dose,' as she called it. But sadly, I make it a practice never to play with the same"—I almost say *meal*—"partner twice. So, I introduced her to him." I sense Leander's stare boring into my back. "It was he who played with her next. Whether they fucked or not is a question best left to him."

She doesn't believe me, or at least, she doesn't want to. When she looks past me to Leander, glimmers of confusion cut through her anger. The puzzle renews. Why is she so insistent?

"Are you honestly expecting me to answer that?" Leander sounds mildly curious. Again, it would take a vampire to hear the tightening anger underneath.

He glares at me. I glare back. An entire unspoken conversation is exchanged in that look.

You can't possibly be serious.

Just answer the question.

You'll take responsibility for the fallout?

Yes.

For fuck's sake. Leander stifles a sigh of impatience. "I did not"—he all but rolls his eyes—"*sully* your sister's…" Stopping, he stares at her and then me in carefully masked and yet increasing irritation. "Nobody even cares about reputations anymore. I have a club to close. Why am I—"

"But you did play with her," I interrupt. Although she tries to hide it, my darling puzzle is nowhere near as adept as we at hiding the hurt she feels at the thought of her sister in either our arms.

"Barely," Leander drawls. "She was… not herself."

All right, now I feel the tickle of two puzzles.

"Not herself?" Merris asks.

Glancing from her to me, Leander comes as close to frowning as I have ever seen him. "She was under the influence."

I almost laugh at him. "Jez had a fondness for vodka, but since when has that ever stopped—"

Now it's Leander's turn to interrupt me. "I'm not talking about alcohol. She had… other things in her system, and I did not care to have them in mine."

I'm surprised.

Merris is furious. She folds her arms tight across her chest, as if that hug is the only thing restraining her from doing or saying more than her tight-lipped, "My sister did not do drugs. Ever."

Leander gives her a look. "Perhaps you didn't know her as well as you think, because when I"—he glances at me—"*played* with her, the girl was high as hell. Deny it all you like—she certainly did—but she was still escorted from the premises. As far as I know after that, she failed the sniff-test twice more and the only night she passed was the night, of course…"

He stops, as if searching for a more tactful way of saying *the night she died*, but Merris had already turned away. She puts her back to us both. Shrugging, Leander gives me a look before he leaves, but I know the rules, and

I know my responsibilities.

I watch Merris, waiting for her to come to grips with what she heard, a little surprised at this lingering fondness for what should have been nothing more to me than another night's meal. I supped at a very beautiful neck, but dinner is over. It's time to send her on her way. Yet, I feel regret. I shall be sorry to see her go. I'd almost like to see her again, but such isn't practical. I'm immortal. Her life is but a flash in the pan. Here for now, but soon to be gone. Getting any more deeply acquainted than this is, quite simply, not worth the inevitable loss.

It's a lesson I've learned repeatedly and well.

Lifting her head, Merris finally faces me again. She truly is horrible at hiding in plain sight. I read the pain that cuts through her, river-deep, as easily as if she were an open book upon my lap.

"What happened that night?" she whispers. "I know she saw you. I know you touched her."

"There is very little to tell about the night your sister died." I am brutally honest with her, although that too inspires a twinge of regret. Her pain at hearing it, however, won't last forever. I intend to make sure of that. "She found me on the dance floor, playing with another. I did not speak to her, there wasn't time. The bouncers removed her from the floor. It was her third strike. The owners here are not fond of drama, so I knew I would not see her again. And yet, there she was, sitting in the alleyway well after closing when I took my leave for the evening. I'm sorry to say but, looking back on it, her being high would make some of her behaviors make sense."

Her expressive face flinched, and she swallowed hard. Shaking her head once, she nevertheless said nothing.

"I offered to take her home," I say, and with slightly more reluctance admit, "She refused. She begged me to give her more, but as I've said, I never play with the same partner twice, and she... well, she did not look well. She was still sitting there when I left. A few days later I heard she died."

She gazes back at me, with wide, unblinking, unconvinced eyes. "You were the last to see her."

My poor puzzle. She needs someone to be responsible, and in her mind, I am it.

So be it.

"Have I upheld my part of our bargain? Is there anything more you want to ask?"

Her hands squeeze her arms. She looks away, but always her gaze comes back to mine. She shakes her head.

Gathering the curtain in my hand, I pull it aside for her. She sweeps past me on a caress of air that smells tantalizingly of apple lotion and the wound on her neck.

Two steps outside this room, she stops so abruptly that I almost run into her back. She's staring, and it doesn't take a genius to figure out at what. Lucy, a club regular, is still bound with her hands to the wall high above her head, but now instead of facing the wall, her back is to it. Her legs are wrapped around Dimitri's waist. He grips her by the ass, fingers digging into the welts he put there. She's grinding on him, and in that flash, I think I detect a whiff of arousal from Merris, even as I feel the sudden thump of her startled heart picking up its beat. She's afraid, not because Lucy is grinding, humping, moaning as she gyrates in the helpless wanting of more, but because Dimitri is feeding. He's bit her. Not once, but several times, and in the red recessed lighting that illuminates them in its devilish glow, her sweet blood flows from multiple punctures for him to lick, kiss and suck.

Merris touches the side of her own neck, her fingers following the edges of the bandage tape I used.

Dimitri is aroused, and while I'm sure Lucy's ass grinding against him might play a part in that, it's the blood trickling from her wounds that's sparked that dim red glow in his eyes. Something more than just a reflection of the lights above us. He isn't being subtle. It isn't his first time feeding from that particular vessel. I fear something more than just personal preference might be at play here, but that's his heartbreak to endure. It only becomes an additional concern of mine when he suddenly senses Merris watching—or perhaps it's her fresh blood he smells. Either way, his head snaps up and that devilish glow as his eyes lock on her is as obvious as the fangs he licks while staring.

Jumping back, Merris slams into me, but I already have her. My hand grabs her arm, the other coming to rest on her throat, forcing her head all the way back onto my shoulder.

"Oh my God," she gasps, but it's all happened so fast, she's still staring at Dimitri. It's several panicked heartbeats later before she notices my hold, and by then my lips are at her ear. My eyes stay locked on Dimitri, making sure he comes no closer. He doesn't, but I can hear the hungry growl rumbling low in the back of his throat as he eyes Merris.

"Wh-why did you stop?" his supper whimpers, dazed.

Licking her blood from his lips, he smiles at Merris before turning back to his willing meal and taking another vicious bite.

One that makes his dinner gasp, then moan, and which would no doubt keep her in turtlenecks for days so no one saw the marks.

Swine.

I let him see my disapproval, but he only laughs. His eyes are still very much on Merris as he feeds, and Merris, poor Merris, her shaking grows more pronounced by the second. She knows what she is seeing, but she doesn't want to believe it. Not any more than she wants to believe I am innocent… at least of Jez's murder.

Then suddenly she notices me. My hand on her throat. My chest against her back and arm gripped tight around her waist, hugging her securely to me.

She twists before I can lock my grip upon her, but she's not trying to break away. Not yet. No, she's staring up at me, open horror beautifying her already lovely face as she searches my mouth. She's looking for the fangs, and God help me, I am enthralled. Once upon a time, we vampires lived on the horror of humans. We lived for the pain, the fear. That BDSM has come so openly to the world has given us an outlet to continue to feed in the manner that suits us best—sweetening the feast with every stroke and cry, our victims becoming supple and willing, well-marinated steaks just waiting for that next bite to be taken. We no longer leave large body counts in our wake, but we aren't half as civilized as we like to appear. And never could that have been clearer to me than in those seconds as her eyes lock on my lips and every-thing in me suddenly aches to show her exactly what I am.

Why not?

I have already fed tonight. On her, no less, but suddenly it isn't enough.

For just one powerfully primal second, I feel newly-sired. The sharpness of my hunger for her is raw, but perfectly paralleled by a secondary hunger, and that one is as shocking to identify as it is unexpected.

Lust.

My cock is hard as hell, sandwiched between her hip and my thigh, and that does not happen for just anyone.

"No fucking way," she breathes, and I smell the aphro-disiac of her fear. If I bit her now, she would probably scream—that lovely, warbling cry of terror I haven't heard in far too long.

No, we aren't very civilized at all.

And I, with my riotous near-adolescent inner lusts all combating one another for supremacy of me, am in this moment, the King of Incivility.

Merris knows what she has seen. I see it in her eyes, the horror that is only sparked by the most unlikely of words—*vampire*. Modern film culture lied to her. We are not the creatures of myth and fantasy that she was led to believe.

"It's all right," I tell her, my pretty puzzle, as I let my mind invade past the delicious panic in her own. "Forget," I whisper, my grip around her waist becoming the only thing that keeps her from falling as I fill her consciousness with my will.

She sucks a deep breath, her eyes widening only an instant before I wipe her mind.

"Need help with that?" Dimitri asks. Lucy looks comatose in his arms, her body has gone limp, her eyes are open, unfixed and staring. She looks drugged, but she isn't. She's flying, soaring in subspace from the combination of orgasm, pain, and the endorphins his aggressive gnawing has inspired.

"Only if you want to die," I reply. He thinks I'm joking. I'm not.

"Next time," he laughs.

There won't be one, not with my Merris.

My will digs in and her mind opens to me like a flower. I love the softness, the lack of multilayered petals created by that well-learned skill called deception. She could not conceal a thought from me if she tried, and locked as she is in my thrall, she doesn't even make an attempt.

I see her memories like flashes of bright color that feel good when I touch them. I do my best to caress them all, identifying them by the varying degrees of emotion and distress attached to each one. Her suspicions are the easiest to find. With a psychic touch, I soothe them. I find her anger and let that go as well. Now she may grieve in peace. I find that shadowy recess that harbors all she has seen, felt and thought throughout this night. It's all so fresh in her mind. So fresh, that I can almost see it, like snippets of a movie reel running in her head. With a bit of reluctance, I erase every trace of me that I can find.

I find the grief and the void that losing her sister has left behind, and I fill it with the only thing I can think of. I tell her there is nothing for her to learn at Club Toxic. I tell her there are no questions left to be answered. I tell her it is a terrible tragedy, but one that Jez would not want her to dwell on. I tell her to go home, grieve and, when she is ready, to move on in her life.

And then, as I withdraw my will from her mind, I tell myself it is time for me to let go too. Tonight has been an unexpected pleasure in so many ways, but I never repeat my play with the same partner twice, and this place is not safe for one such as Merris.

She comes out of the stupor I've put her in as if she's drunk. Incredibly drunk. But, at least she does come out of it. That's always a risk when one goes mind-wiping.

I help her to the stairs, supporting her weight until she wakes enough to get her feet under her again. Her legs grow gradually steadier as up the stairs we go, until by the time we reach the top, she is starting to notice there's an arm around her waist and that I am attached to that arm.

"I don't think you're quite used to whatever you've been drinking," I tell her gently.

"No, I—" She touches her head, looking about the coat closet before twisting in an attempt to see back down the stairs. "I-I guess not."

"I think you were looking for the exit," I suggest. "You found our broom closet instead."

"Oh." She looks down at my arm around her waist again, and then once more back up at me. "Sorry, I—" She stops, her eyes going strange. The pupils expand and her breath catches. Her nipples instantly pebble, thrusting against the fabric of her all-too revealing dress, and the softest, most alluring blush rises to stain not just her face but her chest.

It doesn't take a vampire to detect the gush of wet arousal that would have soaked the gusset of her panties, if only they weren't still lying in a neglected puddle on the floor in the dungeon.

Coming back to herself with a start, she pushes out of my arms. Her mouth opens, only to close again without a word. She takes another hasty step back, but her blush deepens and the peak of her nipples becomes that much more obvious. As if they are reaching out for me, eager to feel the flick of my tongue, or the sharp graze of my teeth as I make my feast of first one and then the other.

It's shocking how easily I can see this woman lying naked before me—beneath me—her pale body covered in the marks of my claiming bite.

Her breath catches again. "I-I have to go," she stammers, just before fleeing both me and the coat closet.

The need to go after her is as appalling as it is irresistible, but after only a few steps, my rebel feet root me to the floor. I watch her go, ducking and pushing her way through the thinning crowd that stubbornly occupies the dance floor. Despite it being well past the 4:00 a.m. closing hour, they haven't shut off the music yet and until they do, the revelers will remain. So will the hunters who prey on them, and there are more than a few.

I watch heads turn, following her as she fights her way to the door, vampire noses and heightened senses pursuing her every step of the way. It's that, I tell myself, not my dissident urges that send me chasing after her. I want only to make sure no one else does. Once I see her safely tucked into the back of a cab and speeding away from here, then and only then will I be satisfied.

Then, I will let her go.

~

Merris

WHAT'S HAPPENING TO ME?

My legs are unsteady. My nerves are vibrating, like the wall I use for balance as I hurry for the exit as fast as I can in so thick a crush of people as are in this place. They're all mashed up together, laughing, dancing, jumping, having a great time. The music is throbbing. So am I, but the tension in my chest says this should be panic, not arousal.

I've got to get out of here.

My heart is pounding harder than the steady thumping bass reverberating through the floor beneath me. Prickles dance across the back of my neck, whispering urgency. I feel watched. I feel followed. I feel horny as hell, and when I look back over my shoulder, all I see are the visions that swept my mind when I looked up into that handsome stranger's face and *saw him with more than just an arm around my waist.*

It was the strangest amalgamation of eroticism and fright. His hands were all over me, peeling the dress—this dress, the one I'm in—from my... m-my sister's... no, no I think it's my body. He's undressing me like a treasure, his mouth never far from my skin. I feel the caress of his kiss following the arch of my neck... the nuzzle that precedes the bite... the sting of his sweet suckling followed by the rush of euphoria. It's like an orgasm that sings through my veins before we fall backwards against a wall that is not like any wall in this club.

I can't see him behind me, but God how I can still feel his kiss on my neck.

I crash into someone, not watching where I am going.

"Sorry... I'm sorry..." I keep pushing, barely glancing up into eyes as blue as they are cold. He's blond, not much taller than I am, on the verge of being just a little too heavy for his frame and he hasn't shaved in days. I used to like that scruffy-rugged look on a guy. Now it seems my type runs to dark-haired, dark-eyed, and handsome as the devil.

Is he still behind me? I twist to look, already dismissing the blond man just as he grabs my arm. My own momentum to get past him swings us both around.

"How the fuck are you still ali—" he says, but after that there's nothing. No sound, although his mouth keeps moving.

It's like time slowing to the crawl of cold winter molasses. Everything I see, everything I hear—it fades away until what's in my mind isn't the dancers in the background or even the grip on my arm tightening until it hurts. It's *my sister hunched in an alley somewhere with her deeply clawed arms hugging her knees and tears tracking mascara down her face as this man lowers himself onto his haunches beside her.*

"Come on," he says in words that echo like they're underwater. *"There's someone I want you to meet."*

The vision breaks abruptly, and so does the blond

man's grip on my arm when my dark-eyed devil grabs his wrist and yanks him around like a doll. I almost fall. It's like my legs have no strength left at all and I can't think.

I have to get out of here.

I have to go home.

I break into a run and slam out the exit. The smell and sounds of the nightclub recede in the background the instant I feel that first rush of cool air wash over me.

I think I must have startled the doorman. He gives me a dark look, but all I know is the freedom of the city sidewalk, no longer cluttered with hopefuls still seeking to get inside, but with those now leaving. They line up just outside the door, waiting for their turn at the taxis constantly arriving and departing. I have to go home. It's the only thought in my head. There's nothing for me here. I *have* to go home.

I've got my arm raised and I'm running toward the busy street, trying to distance myself from the club so I can steal a cab before it gets into line with the others. If not, it'll be twenty minutes at least before I reach the head of the line and can leave. And that's when I hear it, the sudden *pop-poppop* of fireworks. Or the rapid backfires of a really messed up car. That's what it sounds like to me, right up until the rear and back passenger windows of the taxi that's slowing down to pick me both shatter.

A slice of red-hot pain rakes the left side of my body from front to back. At first, I think I've been cut by flying glass. Then everyone starts screaming, and running, and I'm hit from behind, knocked almost flat to the pavement behind the cab for all of the two seconds it takes the startled driver to realize now might not be the best time or place to stop.

Tires squealing, he peels back into traffic, leaving me burning, sliced around the ribs, lying face down on the pavement, and half squashed under the weight of none other than the dark-eyed devil who makes my body sing.

Well… when it isn't bleeding, anyway.

"What—" I try to get my head up off the concrete, but his hand on the back of my scalp makes that impossible.

"We are not a whack-a-mole," he says, forcing my head all the way down onto the ground. It's not until I feel twin jerks of his body, followed by a low growling exhale that I realize what's happening. He's protecting me with his body, and he's just been shot.

Twice.

"Oh my God!" I freeze, grabbing on to his arm with both hands, the one he's using to force me down. I can't see anything except the sidewalk my cheek is crushed up to, the street and the whizzing of tires as cars go racing by a whole lot faster than the thirty-five m.p.h. this part of the city is zoned for.

"I'd pray too if I were you," the stranger atop me growls. "Because if I am still alive when this ends, my darling, you are going to receive one hell of a talking-to."

I don't know why what he just said should evoke such a reaction, but for just a moment, the burning between my legs pulses hotter and harder than the pain in my cut ribs.

He's hit again, and then suddenly it stops. Everything goes silent—but not really. The shooting stops, but the screaming continues. All those people who weren't able to get back into the club before the doorman shut and locked the door, are out here, cowering behind whatever might offer them shelter. The city sounds are still very much all around me. Weirdly, I think I hear the baying of wolves, but also, I hear cars, honking, police sirens in the distance, but coming closer with every shaky breath I take and second that passes. We're practically in downtown Tucson, after all. Nothing is ever fully quiet here, not even in the dead of night.

And yet, in the sudden absence of all that gunfire, everything seems so eerily still. I can hear my breathing; I can hear my heartbeat. I hear nothing from the man lying on top of me. I'm actually starting to fear he might be dead when, slowly, he lifts his head. He pauses, but when no further shots are fired, the weight of him eases back off me, and at last I can move. His is a highly-irritated glare, one that he casts down the street in the direction the shots had come from, then up the other way, toward the wail of approaching sirens, before finally he turns it on me.

As if this were all my fault.

"Where else have you been and to whom exactly have you been asking your little questions?" he demands.

I shake my head, utterly baffled. "What questions?"

A pulse of muscle leaps along his jaw. But up the very long street, a sudden splash of flashing red and blue lights draw his gaze from me and, with mild irritation blossoming into open annoyance, he grabs my arm and drags us both to our feet.

"What are you—" I break off with a gasp when he touches my side, peeling back the torn edges of my dress to get a closer look at my aching side.

"It's just a graze," he decides, but he hasn't let go of

my arm. In fact, before I can do more than gasp again, he bends, grabs the backs of my thighs and suddenly I'm over his shoulder.

"What are you doing?" I shriek, grabbing at the back of his coat for balance when my feet completely leave the ground.

"Kicking myself," he answers dryly. "Not only can I not recover what's already been erased, but Bugattis only come with a leather interior. Try not to bleed all over my seats."

"What?"

He tsks. Catching my chin in his surprisingly gentle hand, he forces me to look at him. "Sleep," he commands.

And just that fast, my consciousness is sucked into darkness.

CHAPTER 5

$\mathcal{M}$*erris*

I DON'T KNOW how fast we're going. All I know is I'm coming out of what feels like a drug-induced haze. My eyes are open. They have been for a while. I'm sitting in the passenger seat of—bar none—the fanciest sports car I've ever seen, much less been in. We are very low to the road. I feel like I'm sitting on it, but while everything outside the window is blurring past us—and, I realize, has been for quite some time now—the ride is so smooth that it seems like we're not moving at all.

My eyes burn, so dry that it stings just to blink. Holding them closed a moment, I roll my weary head the other direction and drink in the sight of the handsome stranger beside me. Tall and lean, well-dressed. He's wearing the caliber of clothing one would expect from someone who drives a car like this. His seat is also pushed all the way back to accommodate the length of his very long legs.

"You're awake," he notices, just a bit too brightly.

I haven't felt this sluggish since coming out from under the anesthesia of my appendectomy back when I was nine. I try to speak, but all I manage is a hum.

"I don't suppose you remember who I am?"

Of course, I do. He's the man who chased me through the nightclub, only to save my life when the shooting started out on the street. He got shot... I think. So did I. I try to look down at myself, but my heavy head drops all the way onto my chest and I almost go to sleep. I flop back against the headrest again, and struggle to keep my eyes open.

He tsks. "My pardon, darling. You may wake up now."

I draw a deep breath, the heaviness in my body seeming to lighten almost immediately. Still, my head is fuzzy and finding a coherent thought is exhausting. "We... we need to go to the hospital," I mumble.

"We'll be fine," he soothes me. "You were only grazed."

With every breath I draw, the haze in my head is clearing, and I'm starting to remember a little bit more. "Did I bleed all over your prized Corinthian leather?"

Casting me a side-eyed smile, he shifts into a higher gear to beat the traffic light before it could flash from yellow to red. "Gaucho, actually, although they tell me the stitching is extravagant. And, no, not that I can tell. If you have, I'm sure the car will survive." Taking one hand off the wheel, he holds it out to me. "Aleron, my darling

Merris. I know you don't remember this, but we are coming to be on quite friendly terms."

Reflexive manners dictate I take his hand, but although habit tries to move me, my arm can't. I look down, puzzled, at the seatbelt. Apparently, he buckled me in, arms, hands, hips and all.

"Ah," he said, putting his hand back on the wheel. "Well, I suppose that's my fault, although I'm not going to apologize. Safety first, darling. You are far too fragile as it is."

"I'm not fragile." It takes effort, but I pry my arms out from under the shoulder and waist straps.

"Compared to me, you are."

Where are we? I look back out the window, watching the blurring scenery as we exit the interstate and head northeast. I don't know when exactly we left downtown Tucson behind us, but we are well out of the city center, heading toward Oro Valley, where cheaper housing gives way to gated communities, which also give way to even better housing. By the time we get to the foothills, they can't even be called houses anymore. These are mansions —adobe spackled walls and red clay tiled roofs, situated on giant tracks of land, carefully landscaped in rock lawns, palo verde trees and Arizona ash, and a colorful variety of desert grass and cactus plants.

"You do *not* live out here," I say as he turns up the winding road into a spacious subdivision, the houses of which all had swimming pools bigger than my apartment. "What are you, a movie star?"

He's amused. "Not quite. Although I feel like one

tonight. I had to drive around aimlessly for some time after leaving the club. For a while, someone was following us."

"Following?" I stutter, baffled. "Why? Who?"

"Those are the million-dollar questions, aren't they?"

We pass two houses, one on his side of this long, curving road, and one on mine. I don't know how long we've been driving or how long I've been sleeping, but it's no longer the middle of the night. The horizon beyond the house I'm staring at, with the shadows of its desert willows like hunched old men standing in the yard, is plum colored. It can't possibly be dawn already, can it?

He turns into the driveway of the next house, and up we wind that way now, leaving the dim garden lights of the fancy properties behind for an unlit stretch of yard that I can't see much of, but what I can see is overrun with cactus.

"Why aren't we going to the hospital again?" I ask, as the house comes into view.

"Because gunshots mean questions," he says, easing up to the garage bay doors.

"We shouldn't have run from the police."

"Police," he says wryly, "mean even more questions and quite possibly over a long period of time. And frankly, I don't have it. Besides, you're going to be fine. Your graze is barely more than a scratch. I promise. I'll take care of it."

Why am I not reassured? Why am I growing more uneasy by the second? All I can think about is home, how far away Tucson is, and in which direction it lies, just in case I should need to start walking. I'm painfully aware that, should I need to call a cab, I don't know where I am or how to direct it to me.

Oh shit, I startle. My phone.

I pat myself down, but I don't feel it slipped down the front of my dress, and I don't see my purse either. Not tucked around the seat or on the floor at my feet. "Where's my purse?"

"There was no purse on the ground when I picked you up. Did you leave it in the club?"

Letting my head drop against the seat, I groan. "Oh my God, no. Shit. Look, I can't be here. I have to go home. Like, I mean right now. I *have got* to go home."

He looks at me, then tsks again, and just as he pauses in front of a garage door which, as if having already sensed him, is rolling open, he turns to face me. "Look at me, Merris."

I do, but inside, I'm already formulating excuses for whatever reason he's going to give me for why I should stay. All except for the one he gives me.

"You no longer need to go home."

The budding anxiousness inside me suddenly eases as a dark heaviness creeps over my thoughts, banishing out everything except the watery echo of his words floating out into every recess of my mind.

And then, as if the world suddenly just snapped its fingers, the heaviness is gone now too.

"Trust me," he says, as if my going home with strange men is a perfectly normal occurrence. "You are far safer here than anywhere else I can think of. I'll take you inside, play doctor to your scratch, give you a comfy bed on which to sleep, in a room you can lock up tighter than Fort Knox. I will even provide you with a phone and a number so you can call Club Toxic and see if someone there found your purse. Now, are there any other issues you can think of? I really haven't got all morning."

"You got shot," I remind him. "Who's going to dress your wounds?"

By now, the garage door is fully open and waiting for us to drive inside.

He regards me with that slight quirk of a smile, but more calculation in his dark eyes than any real amusement. "I'll be fine. It wasn't serious and doesn't even hurt. Here." He holds his hand up, flat and steady for me to examine. "See? Not even the slightest tremor. Were I hurt, at the very least I'd be shaking, right?"

As if sensing him, the house is waking up. One by one, the lights are winking on, casting its much brighter illumination into the car. His hand is steady as a rock. I'm confused. I could have sworn I felt three distinct jolts of impact as he was shot while trying to protect me.

But I hadn't actually seen it happen. I hadn't seen the wounds either, but bullet wounds are bullet wounds, my head is telling me. But then he smiles and lowers his hand onto the gear shift.

"Let's go inside," he says, and so despite my misgivings, that's what we do.

This isn't a house, it's a mansion. In the car, I'd been too focused on him to pay attention to anything else. But as he helps me from the passenger seat, offering me the steady support of his arm as I gasp and groan and hug my burning side, once the pain has subsided enough for me to notice anything beyond it, all I can do is stare. This place is huge—and I'm still only in the garage.

The man has eleven cars, all of them sportscars but one —the oldest of them being a vehicle that is more buggy than automobile, with the top folded down and the steering wheel crowning a very skinny pole that juts up in the middle of a very narrow seat meant for two.

"Mm," he hums, noting my stare. "Mademoiselle has a discerning eye."

"Does that even run?"

"Only when I choose to drive it." He offers his hand. "Boys and their toys."

"You have some seriously expensive toys." I stare in awe as we pass a midnight-blue vintage Porsche, parked beside a stunningly modern silver and black Lotus Exige.

The expense did not stop in the garage. He doesn't live in a house, he lives in a museum. It's cool and quiet, and in every corner, something catches the eye. History and luxury bleed together in the most haphazard example of how someone with more money than sense might live. The interior is modern, with high vaulted ceilings lined with massive wood beams and rock floors polished to a watery shine. The entire front of the house is windows and the furniture is utilitarian and sparse. A Romanesque bust sits upon a Victorian marble top side table where Aleron deposits his wallet, keys and phone. The bust has a Diamondbacks ballcap on its head, and in a wall-recessed glass case directly above it, is a collection of hats throughout history the likes of which I could only identify because what's a girl who stays at home to do except watch a lot of movies?

I see a Sherlock Holmes' hat, a Bowler hat, Zorro's hat, tricorns, World War 1 and 2 military officer caps, a gas mask, three musketeers black-felt hat, complete with red sash and a somewhat worn-looking plume, and a handful of ballcaps all stacked together with the top one sporting a drawing of a hot dog and the words, "That's Mr. Hot Dog to you."

"The bathroom is this way," he says, and I follow him across the living room, past what looks to be an honest-to-God Van Gogh, a wall display of watches every bit as hodge-podge as the hat collection, and down a short hallway. He takes the first door and the bathroom is damn near cavernous. It's huge, with dual square stone sinks and faucets made to look like old yard pumps. The inset whirlpool tub is big enough for six people. The toilet has its own private room. The shower does not— clear glass walls hide nothing of the gray-stone interior with its rain-forest shower head that hits me with a vision the minute I lay eyes on it. It's so strong and real that I can all but *feel the water droplets running off my body as I lift my face into the spray and run my hands through my long, brown hair, rinsing out the last of the silky creamer just as Aleron steps up behind me. The heat of the water flushes his skin, banishing back the paleness as he takes my wrists, pulling me back into his embrace even as he places my hands high up on the wall before me.*

"Bound by my will," he whispers, nipping at the lobe of my ear. I have no idea what that means, but I know what his next command does even as the heady tip of his cock caresses down the crack of my ass, slipping into the

shadowy patch underneath, seeking entrance. *"Tilt your hips back. Shall I take what is mine?"*

"Yes," my vision self whispers.

"Merris?"

I jump, snapping back to the here and now with the phantom pressure of his cock still pushing to enter me as I snap my gaze back to him. The phantom pressure fades, but the heady pulse and throb of my suddenly needy pussy does not. My breasts swell, growing heavy. Heat flushes my face as I catch sight of myself in the wall-length mirror beyond the sinks. I'm blushing, damn it.

And he can't help but notice. Just like I can't help but notice in the mirror that the wallpaper on the wall right behind both me and the still open door is an exact match to the wallpaper I saw in my vision at Club Toxic. That narrow stretch of wall right there behind the door is the place where Aleron will slam me, right before he rips this dress apart in his haste to bare me to his hands, his hungry mouth, and that first breath-taking thrust as he impales what I first thought was my sister, but now know is me on the full length of his pounding cock.

"Merris?" he asks, turning to face me fully now. His head tilts. He looks awfully concerned for what I suddenly know he is. I see it in my head. I see it in the powerful undulations of his body as he fucks me. I see it in the way he grabs my chin, turning my head to bare my neck—a neck that already bears his mark. I see it in the flash of fang just before he bites me, and my wobbling knees almost go out from under me.

I catch the door in one hand and the counter with the other. Because my visions, while sometimes hard to puzzle out, are never wrong. I know what I've just seen will at some point become real, and I don't know what frightens me more: the irrefutable fact that Aleron is a mythological creature that should not exist, or the rush of absolute pleasure that rips through me as Aleron's hungry teeth puncture my neck, his driving cock scrubs me vigorously against the wall, and I come.

Harder and longer than I have ever done before.

I come in the arms of a vampire.

~

Aleron

HER EYES DO that thing again—pupils expanding until all I can see is blackness. She's staring, first into the shower, and then past me into the mirror. I look, but I can't see what would make her suddenly blush and then pale the way she has. She's trembling. Violently. But her nipples are tight little buds that my mouth waters to taste, and she's flushed. That soft pink color I am fast growing to love.

"Merris?"

Her gaze snaps back to me, pupils returning quickly back to their normal size. Her breath catches on a shaky inhale, and she stares at me now the same way that she did at the mirror.

"Show me your teeth," she says, her gaze focusing in on my mouth.

My God. Has she remembered?

Stunned, at first I can't react, not until she suddenly bolts, out of the bathroom and down the hall. And this right here is why I never bring humans to my house.

I almost roll my eyes at myself, and then I race after her. It would be so much easier just to catch her, but I don't. I simply run in front of her and stop—a great blur of motion that to her human eyes magically forms a solid wall of me, right before she smacks into my chest and bounces off. I grab her arm, but only so she doesn't fall. It hurts her greatly. She grabs her ribs, but as soon as she gets her balance back, she's already yanking to free her arm from my hand.

I let her go, holding my palms up in surrender. "Be calm," I say, but she's already running again. Back into the bathroom she dashes, grabbing the door, but I'm still faster. Another blur of motion and I'm behind her even as she's turning to slam it shut between us. Catching the door, I help her hold it shut. Only I'm in the bathroom with her, but that's her problem. I have no desire to continue this dance all the way up into morning. I simply haven't the luxury of time.

When she sees my hand above her own, she snaps around and flattens herself against the door. I smell her fear. The scent of her arousal is every bit as attractive. And those budding little nipples of hers—are they pink? Are they tan? It doesn't matter—beguiling both, trapped behind the flimsy cover of a gaudy clubbing dress that I now know would look vastly better torn to shreds on my bathroom floor.

I halt her next move with a staying hand and a soft-spoken, "Listen to me, Merris."

It's a compulsory thing, the urge to reach into her mind and soothe away everything but her sudden willingness to do exactly that—listen to whatever it is I decide to say next. When one has lived as long as I have, certain skills become second nature. Most vampires can compel—offering suggestions that can often modify a human opponent's next behaviors. The success of the suggestion depends on the age and strength of the compeller, as well as the intelligence and will of the human involved. Old as I am, strong as I am, I have taken suggestions to a whole other level.

I don't just walk through my victim's minds, I dance through them. There isn't anything I couldn't make Merris do right now, but I find myself strangely reluctant to say anything at all. Yes, I want her to calm, but I'd rather she calmed because she knows I won't hurt her, instead of because I've commanded it. If that dress ends up in tatters, I want it to be because she tears it off herself out of desperate wanting for me.

This is strange for me. This desire for willing compliance from someone who should be nothing more to me than another night's supper.

Grudgingly, I lower my hand. Even more grudgingly, I use no mind control at all as I tentatively ask, "Do you want to see my teeth?"

Her gaze flicks to my mouth again.

Oh, this is different. The last time I deliberately showed my teeth, the Bastille had just been stormed, and it was done to scare the piss out of some poor Frenchman right before I savaged him with enough bites to sweeten his blood to that intoxicating level that we all so ache to taste. I truly, truly had been far more intemperate in my youth than I am now.

Not yet sure just how big of a mistake I am making, I bare my fangs as non-threateningly as is vampirically possible.

She stares, her normally expressive face quite mask-like. I'd be quite proud of her if only it weren't so very important to me to know what she is thinking right now.

Her soft gray eyes come back to mine. The very smallness of her is lulling. I am absolutely taken aback by the foreign and yet undeniable need now whispering so seductively in my ear that someone so very small and slight... a combination of enchanting and bedeviling... ought not to go through life without a protector.

As if there has ever been a point in my life when I fit such an absurd definition of that word.

I have to put distance back between us, before I do something stupid. Pushing back off the door, I give her her space.

"Are you going to hurt me?" she asks.

Retreating to the sink, I cover my unease with another smile. "No. In fact, I believe we've already had this discussion. I am going to attend your—"

Wounds gets lost in the bang of the bathroom door hitting the wall, and then she's off again, tiny feet beating a hasty retreat back down the hall for the front door.

I could kick myself.

"Round two," I say, trying not to be annoyed.

I chase after her, but she's got enough of a head start on me now that she actually makes it around the corner toward the garage. She's trying to leave the same way we entered, most likely with one of my cars in her possession.

I duck through one kitchen archway, fully intending to zip through and cut her off at the garage door.

Being able to move as fast as we do has its perks. For instance, who doesn't want to move faster than anyone else in the room? Few people admit, though, such speed also has its drawbacks. For instance, when all of a sudden, the heavy marble bust of a young Roman man swings out in front of me, there is simply no time to stop.

My darling puzzle hit me face first with my own statue, not only breaking my nose, cheek, brow and possibly eye socket, but also knocking me flat on my back. A lesser vampire might have lost consciousness. I am not lesser, and I would sooner hand her my subservient ass on a gold-gilded platter than ever to admit I just lost a few seconds.

Just as soon as I get my wits back, I'll be sure to tell her so.

CHAPTER 6

leron

IF THERE IS anything sadder than a nine-hundred-year-old vampire rolling around on the kitchen floor, holding his nose while his bones slowly knit themselves back together again... well, I can't think of what it is. It might be the pain, but my head is actually ringing. My own blood fills my mouth. It doesn't taste sweet. It tastes annoyed.

Concussion, I think, as I drag myself up the nearest cabinet just so I can get my feet under me. All those protective fond feelings that plagued me earlier are now gone, thank God. Which is good for me, and bodes poorly for her shapely ass the minute I get my hands on her.

Staggering as if at a level of drunkenness I can't even achieve anymore, I grab the walls of the archway just so I don't fall all over myself as I fling around the corner, fully expecting to find her cowering there. Possibly ready now to hit me with the table.

I stumble as the room keeps spinning, but she isn't here. The table is empty and the door to the garage is still closed.

All right. I'll admit it, she's addled me, but I really don't think I lost more than a second or two of consciousness.

Did I?

Almost dreading what I'll find, I manage to grab onto one of the six drifting doorknobs before wrenching the door open. The garage is dark, right up until the motion sensors detect me. The bay doors are closed, and all my cars are there. She isn't out here.

My staggering step is growing more stable as I reenter the house. A quick glance across the living room shows me not only does the front door remain locked, but the yard lights haven't activated. My ears perk. Whispers of movement tell me she's returned to the bathroom, where she no doubt thinks herself safely locked inside. It's well past time, I think, for me to show her just how unsafe she is from me right now.

With every step, my balance returns to normal. Retreating to the kitchen sink, I wash the blood from my face and gingerly touch my nose. Bones tend to take longer to heal, but like bullet wounds, *longer* is a relative term. The tenderness is already starting to diminish. The worst is still around my eye, where I'm sure there might be some slight bruising.

Letting Merris stew in whatever anxieties she might

have over the consequences her rash actions have spawned —because, oh yes, there will be consequences—I head down the hall. I'm more than calm as I walk past the closed bathroom door. I sense her pressed against the other side, listening.

Have no fear, my darling, you will have my attention soon enough.

Continuing on to the master bedroom—which is nowhere near secure enough for me to sleep, but which seems plenty secure enough to house my clothes and toilette—I take off my jacket. Ruined now, of course. Even were it not stained with the blood from my temporarily broken nose, there are still three bullet holes in the back.

Ungrateful minx.

My shirt is ruined too. Both go in the trash. My pants I set out for Consuela, my housemaid who is scheduled to arrive in—I consult my wristwatch—less than four hours from now. I pen her a quick note with listed instructions regarding my uncooperative houseguest, which I leave in the kitchen. Sunup is now in forty-three minutes, damn it. Still plenty of time for me to address matters.

I clean up, change into fresh black trousers and a neatly ironed white shirt, and then I venture into the very back of my walk-in closet. Opening up both cabinet doors, I briefly consult the implements of pain I sometimes enjoy employing whenever I find a submissive capable of taking them. There are worse things at my disposal than just a pair of gloves.

Crops and canes hang neatly on hooks along the inside of the door. I sort through my collection of restraints. Softy that I am, I choose a pair more than capable of holding her, albeit padded ones that won't damage the tender skin of her wrists. I skip the ropes and go straight to chains, which I then padlock to a sturdy wrought-iron post at the foot of my bed. I make sure the length is long enough to reach the toilet in the master bathroom, but nothing that she might use to get herself into trouble while trying to escape.

Because, of course, she'll try. She's a puzzle, not an idiot.

I double check the sturdiness of the bedframe. It's massive, a four-poster draped in thick velvet curtains meant to block out the light, and made of wrought iron not wood. It's heavy as hell. Given enough time, a vampire or a shifter might break out of it, but not a human. She simply won't be strong enough to break the chain or bend the iron bed frame. Padlocking the cuffs together, I then lock them to the end of the chain. I also turn down the covers for her, bringing a first-aid kit from the bathroom to the bedside table—complete with antibiotic and bandages so I can care for her like a proper host. The room is now as ready as I can make it for my darling little troublemaker.

Almost.

Back into the closet I go, where I also skip the severity of my modest collection of rods, ignoring the heavy leather straps and the wickedest of my floggers in favor of a small wooden paddle with a slapping end no broader or wider than the palm of my hand. I really am getting soft to consider so paternal a retaliation, although I doubt she'll agree with that assessment once I have her secured across my knee.

Patting the paddle against my palm, I am decided. I roll

up my fresh shirt sleeves, close up the cupboard, and head back to the kitchen long enough to collect a screwdriver with which to dismantle the bathroom doorknob. I'm just closing the drawer when I hear a knock at the front door.

At this time of morning?

I step back out of the kitchen, take one look at the flashing red, blue and white lights splashing up against my living room walls, not to mention the two uniformed police officers regarding me through the open windows with wary concern.

My darling puzzle. I cast the closed bathroom door a seriously annoyed frown. I really am going to spank her now.

Slipping both paddle and screwdriver into a back pocket, stifling a sigh, I cross the living room to answer the door.

The horizon is gray and only growing lighter by the second. According to my watch, I've less than twenty minutes now and now I have not only two officers on my front porch, but parked halfway down my driveway about a hundred yards from the house, I see an ambulance and a firetruck. Now, I'm seriously, severely annoyed.

"Good morning," I say, mildly.

"Morning," one officer politely returns.

The other is a man after my own heart. He skips the pleasantries entirely and goes straight to the meat of the matter. "We received a call from this address reporting a possible kidnapping. Mind if we come inside?"

"Yes."

The officers exchange looks.

"I understand a warrant should first be involved."

"Sir, we received an emergency call from a woman who says she is being held at this address. Now, we're going to need to ask you to step outside so that we can search the house."

I *really* don't have time for this. Ill-placed fondness may have spared Merris, more than once now, but I have no such feelings for anyone else on my lawn.

"You don't need to come inside," I say, tapping both their minds with mine. "There is nothing going on at this address." *Nothing a stern caning won't fix, anyway.* "You were the victims of a prank. I'm very sorry you came all this way for nothing. Drive safely, officers, and if you would, kindly ask the EMTs not to hit the saguaro cactus on their way out the driveway. It's older than all of you put together, and I admire that."

Letting go of their minds, I retreat back into the house and close the door. I already know how this happened. Still, needing to see the evidence for myself, I walk back across the living room to the short hallway near the garage entrance, where the marble bust that has been my hat rest since I bought it in 1760-whatever now lies broken in three pieces on an equally broken stone tile floor. There is nothing else on the floor amongst the pieces or, indeed, atop the Victorian marble-top table where I habitually leave my wallet, my car fob, and my cell phone.

All three are gone.

I'm pretty sure Merris has them.

Out on the front porch, the officers are coming back to themselves.

"Fucking crank calls," one grumbles as they head back to their squad cars.

"Don't hit the cactus!" the other shouts to the EMTs.

A few minutes later, my walls stop reflecting their flashing lights. A few minutes after that, everyone leaves. After so many years, I feel the approaching sunrise like a physical thing, humming its warning inside me. I don't have time to deal with her. I especially don't have time to deal with my bathroom door.

Shot at or not, I never should have brought her to my home. Certainly, I never should have let myself come to like her and why I still do, after my bust, my floor—*my face*—I have no idea. But there it is, that incredible fondness that right now feels a little like anger and a lot like tolerance, and which propels me across the house to where a single locked door now stands between me and the source of my most recent insanity.

The door jamb splinters all around the latch when I kick it in. I should think anyone stupid enough to call the cops on a vampire and then steal his personal effects would, at the very least, have had the good sense to hide. It wouldn't work. I am so in tune with her, I think I could find her anywhere, but Merris doesn't know that. She also isn't hiding. Standing at the sink, she hugs my cellphone to her chest and stares back at me with those big gray eyes of hers, and a look on her face that says she kind of expected this outcome.

"How exactly," I ask her, propping my shoulder against the now ruined jamb, "do you think I should deal with this?"

"You're going to kill me," she replies without hesitation. "Jez was found with marks like mine on her neck."

My eyes go to her neck. The bandage is not as I originally put it on her. It's crooked, the tape wrinkled. She must have peeled it up long enough to look underneath.

"Did you kill her too?" For the first time, she's not angry when she accuses me. I find I'd almost rather that she was. Despite what she's done—the police, the attack, the incredible annoyance of the whole escape attempt—I find myself poorly equipped to deal with her sadness.

The temptation to reach out and quickly tap her pain away so neither one of us need feel it is very strong. A more sympathetic person might know what to say in situations such as this, but I… I don't have a lot of practice with sympathy.

"I did not harm your sister the night she died. The marks put on her were not mine." Although that did beg the question—whose marks were they? Because when she came upon me on the dance floor of Club Toxic, ranting and clawing at herself, there were no marks of recent feeding to be seen. Nor were there any when I tried to coax her out of the alley later that night.

Someone might have fed on her, but it was not me.

Had that same someone taken one look at Merris at the club tonight and panicked, mistaking her for her twin? Vampires have little need for bullets. Unless shifters or humans are involved, few of us bother with guns at all. We are weapons, and we are much quieter and deadlier in most cases than bullets could ever be. But if the vampire who murdered Jez passed the task off onto a mortal helper… ah now, I think my puzzle has just deepened.

"You've been trying to help me," she says softly.

"Yes," I agree, out of character though it might be for me.

Her shoulders slump. "And I hit you in the face with a statue. Did I hurt you?"

No vampire anywhere would be so stupid as to let a human know they could hurt him. And then there's me.

"Only a little."

"Did..." She winces. "Did I break it? It wasn't... someone you knew, an old friend or something, was it?"

"Well, he's modeled my hats for about three hundred years." I don't know if I should be flattered or insulted that she thinks I'm that old. I steal a glimpse of myself in the mirror. No, I look good. Every inch of me a man in his physical prime—stronger and faster than I ever was before I was turned.

My internal clock is humming, ticking down the seconds to a sunrise that could, in a flash of fire and ash, change all of that if I don't get my handsome ass down-stairs. I should already be there, but I have a problem and I'm looking at her. Based on what she's already done, I'm not about to trust her up here by herself all day long while I'm sleeping.

Nor can I take her downstairs with me. The entrance is secret, and lined with more locks than a vault in the Federal Reserve, but all of those locks open from the inside. I definitely can't trust her to wander about down there, not when I'm comatose and defenseless.

I have no choice and no time left for arguments. Plan A it is. The note I left for Consuela will simply have to do. "Come, I'll show you where you can sleep."

I could gain her cooperation faster if I simply tap her mind and compel her, but just the thought of it tastes sour to me. Besides, when I leave the bathroom, she is still repentant enough to follow me. Or maybe she's just that tired. After all, she's been out with me all night, and the only sleep she's had were those few minutes when I knocked her out.

"Wow," she says, when I take her to my master bedroom. I can see it in her eyes though, she thinks I mean to sleep with her here. "Um…"

Her worries make for a convenient distraction. I move fast, blurring to the bed to grab the chain and restraints before she has even noticed them. I have her right wrist locked into them before she can react, and her left one secured before she can do more than jump back with a startled yell.

She stares at her captive wrists, the thick black leather of the padded cuffs hugging her hands together. Whatever lingering remorse she feeling over her earlier troublesome-ness vanishes.

"What?" she says, holding out her wrists for me to see. As if I'm not directly responsible for it.

"I'm sorry." I'm surprised at how pained I honestly am. Just… not pained enough to let her go. "There is simply no time to arrange for anything else. I will return at sundown."

"What?" she says again, eyebrows arching high. "Wait! You can't leave me here like this!"

Through the bedroom curtains I can see the entire horizon lighting up in shades of orange and yellow. I'm out of time.

"Try to sleep," I tell her, retreating from the room and closing the door behind me.

"*What?*" she shouts, and I hear the rattling of the chain

as she runs after me. But I'm running now too, and by the time I hear my bedroom door bang open—if I see so much as a crack in my wall plaster, I truly will spank her when I awaken—I am already in the garage. The secret access looks like a floor-to-ceiling peg board full of tools. It's sandwiched between two massive tool boxes and unless one knows exactly where to poke it, it won't open. One also has fifteen seconds from accessing the door to disable the fingerprint scanner or the vault door at the bottom of the stairs will shut and lock.

Coolness envelops me with every step I take. The dark-ness is almost black, but my eyes adjust quickly until the peg board above swings gently shut, locking once more into place. A soft light comes on when I set the security alarm inside the room. The vault door shuts, the multitude of clicks as the many locks engage is one of the most comforting sounds I know.

Inside, my internal clock is panicking, even though I am safe now. At least from the sun. I should have been in bed a long time ago. Once upon a time, vampires slept in coffins as a way of hiding from mortals during our most vulnerable daylight hours. A dead person lying in a bed tends to stir alarm. A dead person in a coffin, now that's just business as usual. It's also gone on for so long, that most of my contemporaries still do it.

I, however, never liked the claustrophobic necessity of coffins or even tombs. I have a normal king-sized bed down here. My floors are concrete, the ceiling vaulted, and the air is constantly circulating so it never smells musty or enclosed. It's clean and tidy, and I like the illusion of space.

I can already feel the heaviness of daytime leeching the strength from my body as I kick off my shoes and put myself to bed. I gingerly touch the tender spots on my face as I lie back, but no sooner does my head touch the pillow than does my own weariness forcibly take over.

With any luck, I'll dream of something restful, and not the incredibly troublesome being upstairs in my bedroom.

~

Merris

THE FIT I threw the minute Aleron walked out and left me here, a prisoner in his bedroom, was as brief as it was futile. My ribs hurt, but more than that, it's been a long night and I'm exhausted. The chain and restraints piss me off, but I'm just too tired to do anything more than fall face down into bed and—all right, I sulk first, but then I sleep.

I don't know what time I eventually wake up to the subtle jostle of the doorknob turning, but I know it's no longer morning. My head throbs and my mouth is dry as cotton swabs, like I haven't had water in forever. I don't know if that's a result of getting shot, my thoroughly screwed-up sleep schedule, or the fact that I haven't had so much as a sip of anything for more than twelve hours now. And yet, the instant I see that elderly Mexican woman poke her head in to look at me, I forget everything but her.

Seeing I'm awake, she comes into the room far enough to put the lunch tray she's carrying on the floor.

I scramble onto my knees, thrusting my chained wrists out at her. "Help me!"

Laughing, averting her eyes, seeming horribly embarrassed, she rattles off in Spanish, "*Gracias pero no. No me impliques en tus juegos sexuales.*"

I have no idea what she's just said, but she only shakes her head, patting at me with a staying hand, and quickly retreats again.

On the food tray, she's brought me two bottles of water so cold that condensation is already beading up on the plastic surface. There's also a glass of orange juice, what looks and smells like a sausage-spinach omelet, and buttered toast with two aspirin tablets next to my plate.

I could be an absolute bitch and throw that tray and all its contents after her down the hall, but I'm thirsty, I'm hungry, and my absolute-bitch-bone is severely underdeveloped.

I have more than enough chain to retrieve the tray, and trust me, nothing could ever taste half as sweet as the orange juice I swallow as I knock back those aspirin. I eat everything she brought and finish my meal with an entire bottle of water. The other I hoard, just in case this was the only meal Aleron the Dick Vampire, and my new prison warden, intends to give me.

The throbbing in my head gradually eases. So does the pain in my side. I think I doze off again, and when I snap awake sometime later, the room is slightly darker. The sun's position is over the house now, and my bladder's saying I missed certain key functions the first time I woke up. Fortunately, my chain is long enough to reach the bathroom where I take care of business first and my ribs second. It really was just a graze, although it doesn't make it feel any better as I daub it in antibiotic and try to put a bandage on it.

My chain is also long enough to reach his walk-in closet, where I shamelessly justify my snooping with the knowledge that if he didn't want me in here, he wouldn't have taken me hostage to begin with.

I don't understand how Aleron thinks. Not at all. In the living room, he has veritable shrines set up to his hats, watches, and eclectic art collections. In his bedroom walk-in closet, he has thirty of the same kind of shirt, twenty of the same kind of trousers, eight near identical jackets and eight shoe boxes stuffed with the exact same kind of shoe —black leather, black laces, polished to a shine. It's insane. I can't even begin to compare this to a real closet. For as big as it is, most of the rack and shelf space is entirely empty.

There's a huge wardrobe-style cupboard in the very back. My chain is only just long enough for me to open it with the help of a wooden hanger. I expected to find it empty too, but instead, it's packed full of bondage and implements of sexual torture the likes of which I haven't seen anywhere except what is occasionally used for comedic relief on television or in the movies.

This isn't exactly the social circle I roam in.

Mostly because I don't really have a social life. Apart from a few Facebook friends and people I work with, Jez was the whole of my world.

Nothing in my experience gives me any way to relate to what I'm seeing or the situation that I'm in.

Out in the main bedroom, I hear the door open again

and the elder Mexican lady comes back in to fetch the lunch tray.

"Wait!" I try to catch her. "Help me, please!"

But showing her my wrist restraints only makes her shake her head again.

"No." She blushes furiously, averting her gaze. "*No quiero meter ni hablar contigo ni me interesa tus juegos sexuales.* No sex games, *por favor.*"

Sex games? What? I stand there dumbfounded. "I'm not playing... *really?*" I shake my chains at her. "Call 9-1-1!"

But she's already gone, having closed the door behind her. As far as rescuers go, she's pretty useless, but she did bring me a fresh bottle of water. It's sitting on top of the dresser by the door, already gathering moisture. It's comforting to know I'm not going to be left here in neglect until Aleron decides to come back for me. On the other hand, I really don't think I'm content to wait around until then, like some wilting flower in need of rescue. I'm a modern-day woman, damn it. I'll rescue myself.

I clamber up onto the high four-poster bed, but trying to stand on the mattress is like trying to stand on a cloud of jello. It's very soft and kind of wobbly, although the bedframe itself is heavy enough not to move. Sinking into softness all the way up to my ankles, I gather all the slack out of my chain, plant my bare feet against the mattress and pull. The iron bedframe doesn't break, and neither does the chain. I'm not sure why that surprises me.

Hugging my protesting ribs with one arm, I flop down on my butt, brace both feet against the footrail and promptly spike myself in the toes because the entire wrought-iron frame of the bed is made to look like a rose trellis, complete with black vines and flowers, and even thorns. Lots of thorns, spiking out all over everywhere. I destroy the bedding, ripping back the blankets and wadding them into a thick wedge just so I have a place to put my feet where they won't get punctured as I throw the whole of my bodyweight into pulling on that damn chain. Aleron padlocked the end around two twists of wrought-iron vine and a swirly, thorny loop, and nothing is budging no matter how hard I pull. The lock the chain is bound to is frustratingly solid and so is the rail I'm attached to.

The soft flesh of my fingers aches long before I stop.

I need more leverage.

I'm an ancient Egyptian in the oasis of this bedroom, looking for a fucking fulcrum, and I finally find one. A lattice of trellis bars with thorn-like prongs make up the roof of this bed and hold the heavy canopy curtains in an elegant arch more than four feet above my head when I'm standing on the mattress. If I can lasso some excess chain up over one of those thorny barbs, then like a rope and pulley system, I can increase the force behind each pull, hopefully enough to break free.

The only problem, this bed was made for a giant and my reaching fingers are too short to reach even the lowest thorn. If I stand on the footrail, I might have a chance. Unfortunately, there's a thorny problem with that. Even had I not left my shoes in the bathroom when I tried to call in southern Arizona's Finest to rescue me, I'm pretty sure I'd break both ankles the second I tried to climb up there in heels.

Aleron has shoes in the closet.

Hopping down off the bed, I run to grab a box. It's like playing dress-up in Daddy's Sunday shoes. Even tied down as tight as I can get them, my feet are tiny in these things, but I'm determined. I'm going to make them work.

Except they don't work. Yes, they protect my feet from the thorns, but the vining footrail isn't very wide. Worse yet, the thorns sink into the thick soles of his shoes as I pull myself carefully up against one post and stand on the footrail. There's not time even to turn around before I'm stuck and when I try to lift my foot, pulling up on the over-sized shoe to free it, I lose my balance. It's either leap free of both the stuck shoes and the bed, or break my leg on the way down.

As it is, I nearly bean my forehead on the dresser and the chain makes a horrible clatter catching on various thorns all the way down to the floor.

The shoes are now speared to the footrail and stuck fast.

Okay, Plan B. I'm going to have to rodeo this bastard.

Only now it's not as easy as just climbing back onto the bed, not unless I want the chain that follows me wrapped around a bedpost. I have to get back up over the spikey footrail the way I fell, or I'm screwed.

There's thorns everywhere. Who would ever sleep in a bed like this, much less commission its creation?

Duh... vampire. What does he care if the occupant gets pricked, when every cut's a midnight snack?

I grab the blankets, folding each down into a dense square barrier that would be a whole lot thicker if only I lived in Alaska. In Arizona... blankets are only a thin suggestion. But I pry the shoes off the thorns on the upper part of the railing, and put them on the lower part so my feet have some protection and, using both pillows, I very carefully climb back over the railing the way I'd fallen.

I cut and scratch myself in half a dozen places, including the palms of my hands when the thorns puncture right through the blanket and pillows, but I make it up and over.

I've got to get out of here. I really don't want to have to explain to Aleron what I did to his shoes.

Pulling the length of chain back up onto the bed, I adjust the excess until I've found the middle of it. Searching the iron rose trellis above me, I pick a thorn that's curved at enough of an upward angle to prevent it from accidentally slipping off. It's going to be tricky. The velvet canopy is heavy across the top. So, I'm going to have to throw hard enough to smack the cloth up and, hopefully, get the chain to loop onto the thorn, rather than simply bounce right back and hit me in the head or face.

I start throwing.

I hit myself twice, but I'm determined and—shockingly—on my eleventh or twelfth attempt, I actually hook the chain.

Right in the center of a single link.

Which promptly slides straight down onto the curving thorn, becoming stuck there.

"Are you fucking kidding me?" I shake the chain, trying to ripple it back up and off. As near as I can tell, though, I only stick it farther. I didn't even manage to get the chain caught up there in the middle of its twelve or fifteen-foot length. Oh no, I'm hooked to the roof of this thing, chained by the wrists on a leash that's only four or so feet long.

I can't even sit down anymore now without stretching my arms to their absolute limit.

Damn it.

CHAPTER 7

$\mathcal{M}$erris

I FEEL LIKE A FISH, dangling from the fisherman's line, with absolutely no hope of rescue and nothing to do except watch through the crack in the bedroom curtains as the sun slowly sinks.

I can't even see it anymore. My window faces east. But I can see the hue of the sky changing colors, gradually deepening, the baby blue of this beautiful day turning the color of a bruise as it darkens. I have no idea how long I've hung here, alternately switching between standing and dangling with my arms pulled straight up. I think it's been hours, the molasses-slow passage of time occasionally punctuated by the increasingly mortified housekeeper wandering in and out.

I don't know which of us my change in predicament has embarrassed more. The first time she saw me in it was when she brought a supper tray. She looked at the chain, at the thorn, shook her head as she looked at me, and then climbed up onto the bed alongside me.

"Help me," I begged, but she only put half a turkey sandwich in my right hand and an uncapped water bottle in my left, and climbed back down again. "Don't go!" I cried.

"No involve sex games!" she replied, almost as desperately.

And so, with nothing else to do, I ate my stupid sandwich, drank my stupid water, and I hung there while slowly the sky got darker. The purpling bruising hue turned grudgingly inkier and the shadows inside my room grew longer. I stood up. I sat down. I wished I'd been smart enough to turn a light on, because now I was sitting in the dark.

I also wish I'd not drunk so much water or had the foresight to visit the bathroom before hanging myself up like this. I really have to pee.

The house goes quiet. Not that the elderly woman who'd been taking care of me all day had made a lot of noise, but occasionally I heard her. I know she cleaned up the mess I made with Aleron's bust. I also heard a vacuum in the distance. One of the times she brought me water, she puttered through the room long enough to clean the bathroom and, although she looked longingly at the bed, she left again without touching it.

I could maybe understand it if I thought she was frightened. Does she know she's working for a vampire? *Surely,* she has to know something about this whole situation is odd. She *has* to. But now, every time I see her, the impression I get isn't one of fear. It's one of incredible embarrassment.

I'd like to think if I'd walked in on something like this, I'd let a 'fish' go, but there's no telling what Aleron's told her or how often that poor woman comes to work to find something like this going on.

The thorns are on this bed for a reason. The nape of my neck prickles as I regard them in the failing light and try my best to pretend my nipples aren't prickling too. What in the hell does he use them for, and am I about to find out?

The longer the silence stretches on, the worse the prickling gets. This right here is why wild animals would rather chew off a paw than keep waiting. With each new star that winks on, I'm getting closer to that moment when I know Aleron is going to come for me. Surely, he has to be awake by now.

What's taking him so long?

My ears prick. Was that a whisper of sound I just heard, the soft scuff of a hard-soled shoe on polished stone floors?

I was wrong. *This* is why animals chew their paws off. *This*, this heightening sense of impending doom that now crawls up my back to dig with thorny claws into that warning spot between my itching shoulder blades. I tug. It's pure reflex, and quite hopeless. If I could have worked my hands free without dislocating both thumbs, I would have hours ago.

I'm a wimp when it comes to pain.

—Aleron's arm slipping around my waist, pulling me back into the embrace of his hard body as his other gloved hand slides down between my legs, pricking my mons, my

folds, my clit in the most exquisite combination of ecstasy and discomfort—

My traitor's body doesn't care how long I've hung here. All of a sudden, all I feel is the aura of him, pausing at the other bathroom where he lingers—to shower, to warm his skin long enough for his hands to feel normal when he touches me?—before continuing on to the kitchen.

I smell coffee. The unmistakable sizzle of bacon. Toast.

He's wending his way closer, coming to me now, and I feel it with such seductive certainty that even without a whisper of sound to betray him, I know he's there a half second before the door latch turns.

The door pushes open and there he is, haloed in shadow. As far as I can tell, there isn't a single light on anywhere in the house, and yet I know he can see me. I can damn near hear the quirk of his smile a half second before he turns on the bedroom light. He has a breakfast tray for one balanced in one hand, and the look on his face is completely unsurprised. He looks at me before his gaze follows the chain up to the ceiling.

"In about two seconds, I'm going to pee your bed," I say. I'm trying not to sound petulant, but I am not amused.

Putting the tray on the dresser, he climbs up onto the bed, fishing a set of padlock keys out of his trouser pockets. He takes each of my wrists in turn, freeing me from the cuffs and sparking such a thrill from his touch alone that I am instantly and irrationally annoyed.

"Pervert." Jumping off the bed, I run to the bathroom

with his low chuckle teasing me all the way. "What did you tell that poor woman?"

"That you and I have a bet going on whether or not you could break free before nightfall."

"Bullshit!" I call through the closed door. "She thought we were playing sex games!"

"That's because I asked her not to be here when I 'got home,' since I didn't plan to be quiet about taking my prize once you'd failed. Have you any idea how much a pair of Brunello Cucinelli shoes cost?"

I emerge from the bathroom after washing my hands. "Like you don't have seven more just like them in the closet."

"That's hardly the point." But he's still smiling, shaking his head, chuckling at the condition of my chain and the bed even as he pries his shoes off the thorns. He looks at the holes in the soles.

"I hope it rains every time you wear them." Folding my arms tight across my chest, I glare at him.

He's not offended. He does, however, throw the shoes in the bathroom garbage. "Are you hungry?"

I'd love to tell him no, but I am quickly finding out I am nobody's bastion of iron-willed resistance.

"I brought cream and sugar for your coffee," he coaxes, but I've already broken. It's as if he's left me to starve for days, rather than hours. I attack the tray he's brought and eat as fast as I can, standing up at the dresser. Bacon, eggs, toast and defeat never tasted quite so good. "I'll want to take a look at your wound when you're done."

"Ha!" In two bites, I've finished off one slice of warm

toast. "You left me chained in this room all day. Right now, I could care less what you want."

"Come now, don't hold grudges," he says mildly. "It doesn't become you. Besides, you broke my nose and my bust, and brought police to my front door."

"I never asked to come here."

"I never asked to get shot three times, and still I have a bullet lodged against my ribs. I can't begin to tell you how little I relish the thought of cutting it out later on."

"The mood I'm in, be glad I don't have a knife. I'd help you." I take a bite of crispy bacon, but I've forgotten one very important thing. The man I'm sniping at isn't a man. When he wants to, he can move so much faster than I could ever hope to counter.

I don't even hear him move. One minute he's at the bed, and in the next, he's across the room. His large hand clamps onto my wrist and the whole room spins as he swings me around. My back bumps up against the now closed bedroom door and the weight of him presses me to it. The wedge of his knee is suddenly wedged between mine, not just forcing them apart, but scissoring all the way up between mine until his thigh bumps my pubis, lifting me up until my toes can barely find the floor.

I grab his shoulder with my free hand. He has my other wrist, once more making a captive of the hand that still holds my last bite of crispy bacon.

Slowly, with ridiculous ease, he forces my hand to his lips. He smiles. His eyes neither blink nor leave mine, not even when he opens his mouth and—to my supreme annoyance and the single, heated thump of shamed arousal that pulses through my pussy—he makes me feed him.

"I didn't know you ate real food." My voice doesn't tremble, but the rest of me does, particularly when he takes each of my fingers into his mouth one at a time and licks the lingering taste of bacon from each one.

"You might be surprised at what I'd enjoy eating."

I really am trembling now. "You mean me." I hike my chin. "Is that what you're going to do with me now, suck me dry?"

"Oh, darling, I dearly hope not. Done right, the last thing you should be is dry."

My cheeks burn and, damn it, those low thrumming pulses have set my pussy to throbbing beyond my ability to ignore. I have no defenses against this. With every breath, my breasts caress his chest, and with every beat of my own treacherous heart, my clit throbs against his thigh.

"Then again," he says, tipping his head at an inquiring angle, "pleasuring you is the last thing I should be contemplating considering all your naughtiness. You have no idea how close you came last night to a good old-fashioned spanking. Had I only the time, you would even now be wearing my marks on more than just your pretty neck."

No one's ever told me I had a pretty neck before.

Of course he would, idiot. Remember the fangs.

Shaking my head, I flatten myself against the door and shut my eyes tight.

"What are you doing?" He sounds amused.

"Get out of my mind," I say through tightly clenched teeth.

He laughs, a breathy sound that brushes my face with coffee-scented air. "I am not in it. Yet." The heaviness that settles over me as his gaze bores into mine is instantly both ominous and intoxicating. I breathe in, my gasp at his mental invasion cut short. "Now I am in your head."

I cling to his shoulder, my hand holding fast to the back of his neck, and only belatedly do I realize I haven't even tried to push him away. I breathe in when he does, and I know what it is he's scenting for because it's there, molten trickles of hot wanting that flow down through the folds of my eager sex to soak into the dark fabric of his trousers.

"Do you want me, my darling Merris?" he asks, silken as the devil.

I have never wanted anyone half as badly as this. I twist my head away, not even realizing I've just bared the vulnerable, unbitten side of my neck to him. Before I can undo the damage, he has already bowed his head. His exhale is cool against my skin as he follows the defenseless slope, his mouth never more than a kiss away.

"Open," he says, and I do. Both my eyes and my legs, and I don't even realize the heaviness isn't even in me anymore until he pauses to press a kiss upon my jugular and then raises laughing eyes to mine. "You did that of your own volition. While I did touch your mind to show that I could, I have not compelled you to do anything. Do you want me, Merris?"

He doesn't speak my name so much as he purrs it. The very sound of it on his lips shivers me. I want so badly to shake my head and tell him no. Even more, I wonder what his kiss might feel like with a little nip of fang tugging at my bottom lip.

～

Aleron

I'M NOT WEAK. I don't tremble, but I must admit I do so love the feel of Merris sitting upon my thigh, her lithesome body sandwiched between me and the door, shaking. I smell her lust. It's firing my own and, frankly, it's been so long since last I felt this particular appetite that I can barely restrain myself.

Let go, I think. *Nothing good can come of this*. It's a lesson I've learned more times than I care to recall and yet, I can't seem to make myself obey. The bow of her pink lips is a seduction I do not care to ignore. I'm going to have to change my trousers because her panties were left on Club Toxic's floor and the wetness of her silken arousal burns into my leg. That's a heat I would dearly love to get lost in.

"Do you want me, Merris?" I ask again.

She looks at my mouth as I say it. She wants to say no, but when she parts her lips, no sound comes forth. She aches to say yes. Aches, I decide, should always trump wants, and I kiss her.

I have kissed a thousand women in the years since I've become civilized. I've killed so very many more, but even when feeding was not the motivating factor behind each amorous display, I rarely feel anything beyond the pleas-antness of living, human warmth pressed up against me.

What I feel with Merris I have not felt in ages. I don't know if I have ever felt it. This is more than hunger. It's more than biology, and frankly, my personal biology has been so unbelievably fickle as of late that I can hardly believe how readily it rises to the occasion that is her sweet body arching into my touch. She is an innocent eager for more, and I would give it to her.

My hand is on her breast before I know it—a perfect fit within my palm. The needy tip of her nipple responds to the rolling caress of my thumb. It stiffens fast to my gentle tweak. She catches her breath again, not quite muffling the soft moan that escapes her when I lightly—at least at first —twist.

Her grip on the back of my neck tightens. It tightens even more as I break the kiss to catch her bottom lip between her teeth. I let her feel my fangs, but I am careful. I don't bite. Not yet.

Taking both her wrists, I place her hands against the door just above her head. "You are bound by my will. Do you know what that means?"

She is visibly shaking, but her face is flushed and her lips slightly swollen from the passion we have shared. A tiny side to side movement indicates no. She is watching me like a virgin, at a complete loss for what to do.

I've never much cared for virgins and yet, my fondness for this one deepens the harder she trembles.

I explain, "It means you must hold this position, the one I have put you in, until I say you may move. If you disobey, everything stops. Do you understand?"

She nods her head up and down, an even smaller, tighter motion than before.

I press her hands a little harder, cementing them in place with nothing more than a look. "Bound by my will," I say again.

She shivers, but when I let go of her arms, she keeps

them exactly as I've put them.

My lovely Merris, the mystery that so intrigues me.

I lower her gently back onto her own feet and reluctantly remove my leg from between hers. Immediately she shifts her feet closer together, but stops when I look at her. Technically, she's broken the rules already, but the look that crosses her very expressive face is one of instant confusion.

"What are you doing?" I ask her.

Her gaze flicks sideways, as if the answer lies somewhere off to my right. "T-trying not to fall?"

"Did I say you could move?"

Her cheeks pinken all over again, but with hesitant obedience she widens her stance again.

I lean in to her, bracing my forearms alongside her own against the door. Our faces are very close. My eyes level with hers, I share her shivery, uncertain breaths.

"Did," I pointedly repeat myself, "I say you could move?"

Not daring to look away, she shakes her head.

"Out loud, if you please."

"No."

"No, what, my naughty darling?"

Her brows quirk and her blush deepens, my endearment embarrasses her. She swallows hard, but she eventually makes herself say, "No, sir."

I like the way that word looks on her lips. Humming, I kiss her slowly, savoring the taste of it there while her softly hitching breaths turn into helpless moans, and her shaking intensifies all over again.

"I think I would prefer the term Master." It's not one

I've held for a long, long time, although it is one I've ached to hear from her practically from the moment I first saw her.

Her eyes are unfocused, a smoky storm of gray that follows the motion of my mouth. I haven't compelled her, but she obeys as if I have.

"Y-yes, um… Master." She blushes furiously once she realizes what she's said. Her brow furrows. She's embarrassed, confused, hopelessly aroused, and she doesn't seem to know why she has agreed to say it. So, I give her a reason.

Taking hold of her dress, I rip the ruined garment from neck to hem, and in a single yank, her beautiful body is completely bared to me.

She stiffens in shock, her eyes going huge, her flushed lips rounding. She doesn't protest, though. Mostly because I don't give her the chance. Discarding the dress to the floor, I cup her naked breasts in my hands. My fingers conquer one jutting tip, while my mouth consumes the other.

Her back arches and in her desire, she forgets the rules. She grabs my shoulders. It's a serious infraction, but one she instantly corrects herself. Snapping her hands back to the door, she whispers hoarsely, "I'm sorry. I didn't mean to, I'm sorry."

Raising my head from her breast, I look at her.

Her expression melts into a longing wince. "M-Master?"

Well, there's no such thing as a perfectly trained submissive the first time one plays.

"Don't let it happen again," I warn.

She shakes her head against the door. "No, I won't."

Drawing back, I deliver her first taste of discipline. A sharp upward slap to her sweetly-suckled breast which catches the wet tender nipple with force enough to make her knees buckle. She sags against the door, her gasp shrill with surprise.

"No, what?" I ask, exaggerating a level of patience I don't often bother to exercise. But then, she inspires from me all sorts of out-of-character behavior.

"Master!" she gasps as I slap the other breast in turn. Her whole body stiffens in dreadful anticipation when I drop my punishing hand down between her thighs.

I slap her little clit too, but nowhere near as hard as I have her naughty nipples. I also don't stop at one. I spank her dear pussy briskly, repeatedly, my blows barely harder than the gentlest of pats, but on a place so sensitive and aroused that I don't need much force to soon have her writhing against the door.

She grabs her own hair to keep her hands up. Her thighs are quaking, but she keeps them well parted.

"Good girl," I purr, proud of her for not snapping them shut. I take her pussy in hand, squeezing just hard enough for her to realize what this is. This is ownership. This—hot moisture spilling from her onto my fingers—is mine.

I hold her gaze as I lower myself to my knees. Hers is a wondering stare, tinged with equal parts lust and uncertainty.

"Bound by my will," I remind her.

She flattens herself to the door—all that lovely stubbornness now focused on nothing but obedience. That pleases me. So does her reward.

Parting the folds of her with my fingers, I drink in my first taste. The heat of her is luscious, the intoxication of all that hot, sweet blood pulsing through her swelling sex an aphrodisiac beneath the lash of my tongue and the kiss of my lips. I feel the pulse of her blood, the beat of her heat, the burning of her mounting desperation as she writhes, grinding her hips into the motions of my mouth.

The well of her sex weeps upon the thrust of my longest fingers—first one, then two—stretching her open while all that wet slickness drips into my palm. I feel the spasms, the milking, quivering motions of her sex as I lock my mouth upon her clit and suckle without mercy. I drive her hard and fast, not content to bring her merely to the edge of orgasm, but hurling her off that ledge into the gyrating fury of a climax that all but makes her dance against the door.

That's when I bite, releasing that rush of endorphins that turns her shout into the most guttural of moans. I press her hips flat to the door with one hand, preventing her from bucking, riding, and grinding into each of my feeding draws—preventing her from tearing her tender flesh on my sharp teeth. With my other hand, I fuck her vigorously, feeling the ripples of her seizing flesh as she comes again.

I know better than to feed on her again so soon, so I give myself only the sweetest and briefest of tastes. One that has now left my mark in a place only another lover will ever see again. The very thought of that is so unpleasant that I'm instantly tempted to bite again—and again and again, if necessary, marking her sex in puncturing 'mines' that only another vampire would recognize.

And probably ignore. Too many of our petty amusements consist of deliberately vexing one another.

Forcibly restraining myself, I lick instead, gradually coaxing the bleeding to stop as I make her ride every last shuddering wave until she collapses, panting and whimpering against the door. Her legs are shaking so badly that she nearly sags all the way down to the floor, even as I rise back to my feet.

The taste of her dominates my mouth. I can't stop licking my lips.

"That is another wound I'll need to be mindful of." I struggle to pull my rampaging passions back under firm control. "Was your breakfast satisfactory?"

Her eyes are half closed, her face calm and flushed and positively glowing in pleasure's aftermath. "Was yours?" she returns huskily.

Minx.

My exhaling chuckle sounds more like a growl. She has no idea how close she is to being bent over the nearest and sturdiest piece of furniture and fucked until I've exhausted myself in her beautiful, fluid heat.

"Clean yourself," I order her instead. "I shall return in ten minutes to attend your wounds, after which we are going to leave."

That gets her attention. She looks at the puddle of her torn dress on the floor, and then, incredulously, back at me. "Where are you taking me now?"

"Home. Your home." Drawing her off the door, I turn her in the direction of the bathroom and give her a gentle swat to get her moving. "It's past time we found out who tried to kill you last night, and why."

 leron

THE PASSAGE of time is a funny thing. For the vast majority of my everlasting life, I have watched while we, as a species, made minor advancements in life, war, medicine, science—our basic understanding of this world in which we were created to live. Apart from a minor burst of invention here or there, pretty much from the moment I was born—the spoiled lesser son of a nobleman—and then sired—a soldier seeking glory in war-torn Antioch in the fall of 1097—we have stayed evolutionarily stagnant. It's only been in these last hundred years or so that human advancement has exploded to such a fascinating extent.

Cars.

Computers.

Telecommunication.

Human beings leaving the atmospheric pull of the earth to walk in manmade facilities among the stars.

Human beings on the moon.

Velcro.

And yet, as I speed up the interstate back to downtown Tucson, with Merris dressed in naught but her high heels and one of my shirts, I find myself struck by a singular realization. For all our gadgets and newfound scientific knowledge, one thing has not changed. Not in all the times that I have seen it, throughout the stretch of my incredibly jaded life—nothing beats the sight of a woman wearing a man's shirt.

Poor Merris, she's very nervous. She's swimming in the pristine white fabric, constantly fidgeting with the unbuttoned sleeves that are too long for her arms by at least six inches, repeatedly checking to make sure all the buttons are buttoned and that the hem is as low over her thighs as she can make it go.

"I really need clothes," she says, not for the first time.

"No one will see you, darling," I assure her. "Not if I don't want them to."

And this is not a visage I am inclined to share, not with anyone. Still, it's not until we pull into her apartment complex that I see why she's nervous. I used to hunt in places like this. It's my first thought as I look around the compound of old brick buildings with its crumbling adobe façade and whitewashed 'security' fence, streaked with spots of amber rust bleeding through the paint. It's not quite a slum. The buildings date themselves somewhere around the 1950s. There's water in the community pool, exercise and laundry facilities, and even massive air conditioning units that click on as I park the car as close to her building's entrance as I can get. But still, in my mind, at first all I see is London's East End, Russia's Tolyatti, damn near anywhere in France right before the explosive rise of the revolutionists made it so very easy to add to the body count. War and dissidence used to be a vampire's best friends. So was poverty, but then, of course, we got civilized.

Compared to what I've seen in the past, this is almost palatial, but—I find myself thinking—nothing like what I could provide for her. Were I so inclined, of course.

Which I'm not. Because, don't be ridiculous.

I've already broken my personal rule about playing twice with the same woman. I'm already having a difficult time thinking of her simply as supper. It's the shirt, I think wryly. She really does wear it exceedingly well. It's all I can do, when I glance at her, not to lick the tips of my fingers and reach down between her legs, beneath the hem of all that pristine whiteness, and see if I can make her come again. Despite the tenderness my fangs left upon her tasty nether folds. Not to mention her existing unease.

Shutting off the car, I would have done the gentlemanly thing by holding her door and offering her a helping hand out. Braced for a night of incognito sleuthing, I'd decided to exchange the Bugatti for a far more subtle Ferrari LaFerrari, fire engine red with doors that fold up like butterfly wings. I do so love technology. But I'll also be the first to admit I didn't quite think this through. The minute the car stops, Merris is out and sprinting for the door as fast as she can go while holding the button-down skirt of my oversized shirt closed in front and down in back.

To say we attract attention would be something of an understatement. Night it might be, but it's not so late that people aren't out and about, gathered on their balconies and chatting on the stoop. There's a perking curiosity that my car stirs just by existing in this parking lot. I doubt anyone even notices Merris, kicking out of her heels the second she gets the main door open. She barely holds it long enough for me to catch up, and then she's sprinting for the stairs again, all bouncing breasts and sexy bottom barely hidden behind the tail of my shirt.

I like following her. The view is almost worth saying goodbye to all four hubcaps.

That view is also the reason I didn't notice the familiar and very faint scent of living death the minute I walked into this place. I am all the way up on the second-floor landing, just rounding the bannister to watch as my darling Merris grabs the top of the third-floor rail to swing herself around into the hallway, when suddenly it's not just in my nose, it's tickling at all my senses.

The scent is strong.

A vampire wasn't just here at some point tonight. Whoever it is, he still is.

Merris

I DON'T THINK I've ever taken the stairs so fast before. All

I can think is—just get home, get inside, get clothes on. I've just reached the top of the third-floor steps, when Aleron's rushing blur cuts me off faster than I can stop. I crash into him and might have fallen backwards right back down the stairs had he not caught me. His arm is like a steel band around my waist, hugging me close as a lover. Which... I guess we kind of are, considering what he did to me over a few snarky comments and a half slice of bacon.

My nipples peak. An Arizona rose of heat unfurls inside me, igniting in all the places where his fingers and mouth had touched me. It's mortifying how wet I get in so very short a time.

Motionless apart from the flaring of his nostrils as he breathes, he says, "Not now, darling."

Oh my God, he can't possibly have smelled that, could he?

He pats my head. "Stay here."

I stare after him as he leaves me standing at the mouth of the stairs, eyebrows slowly crashing down over my glaring eyes.

Asshole.

I march after him because, first, I'm not a dog, and second, nobody that I have to live with in this building needs to see me doing the walk of shame in a rich man's shirt when I'm supposed to be grieving. I already feel guilty as hell. I don't know what possessed me to go to Club Toxic in the first place. It's like I've got giant holes in my head where explanations for all of last night's actions ought to be, but I can't remember how those holes should be filled. Perhaps I went there hoping to feel close to Jez in a place I know she used to love. I don't know. I can't explain it to myself, the last thing I want to do is to feel backed into a situation where I have to justify it to others.

Like Ms. Menendez—otherwise known as Saguaro Canyon's very own town crier—who lives across the hall from me. *Please, dear God, don't let her come shuffling out to talk to me tonight.*

Just the sight of my door, the last apartment next to the emergency exit at the end of the hall and the giant window that overlooks the parking lot, reignites my need to hurry. And yet, not only is Aleron blocking the hall so I can't squeak past him, but he's heading right to my door. I never told him my apartment number.

"How do you know where I live?" I ask, but his hand snaps up, both halting and silencing me.

He ventures closer, his upraised hand becoming a single, staying finger. His movements are as silent and as graceful as they seem suddenly quite deadly. That's when I notice my door stands cracked open. More than that, it's not just cracked, it's been kicked in. I can just make out the splintered wood where the deadbolt used to latch.

My shocked step forward is as involuntary as, I think, Aleron's response. He catches me, his open hand coming to rest on my stomach, stopping me mid-step. He doesn't look at me, not even when he raises a silencing finger to his lips. His head turns. He's listening, tracking movements so soft that I can't make out so much as a whisper.

"You may as well come in," a man calls out from inside my apartment. "I heard you coming up the stairs, and I could smell her all the way from the lobby."

Aleron's face has no discernable expression, apart from a tic of muscle as his jaw clenches. I look down when his finger taps my stomach, but I don't think Aleron knows he's doing it. He's thinking, but only for a moment before saying to me, "Stay right behind me. Do not speak, and do not move more than a step from my side. Is that clear?"

I nod, the flesh of my neck crawling as I take my place behind his muscular frame. Slowly, he pushes my broken door open, but I'm looking down the hallway, back the direction in which we've come. I see nothing. I hear nothing. I've lived in this building for two years, and I don't think I've ever seen the place so still or so quiet, even at nine o'clock at night.

I glance behind me. Ms. Menendez's door has been kicked in too, but pulled closed just like mine was. A tiny smudge of reddish brown no bigger than a thumbprint marks the doorknob. I stare at that, completely unprepared to make that next logical leap. Ms. Menendez is always home. She never leaves, not even to get groceries, and she would never tolerate so much as a smudge on any part of her door. She's in the hall almost every day, scrubbing it and grumbling about the kids from two doors down who use this hall as their personal playground.

Oh Jesus, has every door on this floor been kicked in. Why is it so quiet?

That spot between my shoulder blades itches unbearably. I feel sick, rooted here in the hallway as Aleron eases no more than a step across the threshold, already looking right, toward my tiny enclosed kitchen.

"I believe you are in the wrong apartment," he says to whomever he finds inside.

"No, this is the right apartment." The soft thump of my purse hitting the floor at Aleron's feet sounds obscenely loud in the unnatural quiet of this place. "I'm absolutely in the right place. It's you I'm concerned about, my friend. Wrong place, wrong time, definitely the wrong girl. Company makes the man, and all that. Sometimes it can even get him killed. Walk away."

"Not a chance." Aleron turns his body toward the kitchen, blocking the doorway, but otherwise he doesn't move.

I do, though. Pulled by the most dreadful, icy feeling, I creep the few steps that separate my door from my neighbor's. My fingers tremble as I reach out. It only takes the softest touch of my fingertip and the door swings slowly in.

Her apartment is every bit as clean as her door. Spotless, brightly decorated in ceramics and a veritable jungle of living plants that bush from every corner, on every available surface. The patio drapes are wide open. A single light is on, a bright reading lamp on the table by the recliner where Ms. Menendez is. At first glance, one might think her sleeping. But she isn't, and I know it even as I try to convince myself otherwise.

Her eyes are open, her head tipped so far back and cocked at a broken angle. Her legs are sprawled apart. So are her arms, each draped over an opposite arm of the recliner, with wrists turned up, making the fang marks on them easy to find. Her neck looks gnawed, the flesh torn and mauled.

She is not alone.

An older, masculine figure sits on the loveseat reserved

for company. Another steps slowly out of hiding to stand in the archway of her tidy kitchen.

The itch at the back of my neck has grown terribly. I look right, back down the hallway in which we've come just as another figure steps soundlessly out of another apartment. And then another one. And another. Four more men, one from each of the four other apartments that crowd this floor.

"Welcome home, Jez," the man on the couch calls to me, and my eyes snap back to him. He's mostly bald, with little more than a wreath of sparse gray that wraps his skull from ear to ear. When he stands, he's not particularly tall and almost seems frail until he moves a step toward me, then stops. I hear the breath he takes as he lifts his nose, scenting the air. Like a dog, I think.

Or a vampire.

Seven vampires—two in this apartment, one in mine, four moving in like assassins down the hall—Aleron makes eight. I feel him behind me, his cool hand light upon the back of my neck.

And then there's me, just standing here, staring dumbly with no place to run—as if any human could ever hope to move faster than a vampire—except out the fire escape, and what's the chance of there being one or more vampires out there, just waiting for us to attempt it.

"You aren't Jez," the man says, mildly surprised. He laughs, a soft, breathy sound. "I am such an idiot. You're Jez's sister. Her twin?"

"Yes," I whisper with a nod.

The shadows in Ms. Menendez's living room have carved hard angles in the lines of his narrow face, and yet when he smiles they seem almost to soften. "I'm sorry. I didn't know, but I should have. How very unfortunate for you."

He looks friendly. Sympathetic. He looks like someone's kindly old grandfather, even as he tells the dark-skinned vampire filling up the kitchen archway, "You may kill her now."

Everything up to that point seems so slow moving. So still. The incredibly deadly calm that one only fully appreciates right before the storm suddenly explodes all around them. This storm hits harder and faster than my eyes can follow or my mind can register, because the next thing I know I'm on the floor, flung there by Aleron's shoving grip on the back of my neck. I still feel the warning flex of his fingers closing over my nape, that phantom grip has my nerves stubbornly insisting his hand is still there when the window overlooking the parking lot shatters. I flinch, barely glimpsing the blur of the vampire from Ms. Menendez's kitchen flying backwards out through it.

I suck air, but the blur of the vampires coming up the hall became nothing more than bowling pins falling all over one another as the vampire from my apartment slams into them.

"Sh—" is what I have time to shout before the blur of Aleron's arm locks around my waist, lifting me clean off the floor. He cradles me like an infant, his other hand pressing my head to his shoulder, and it's probably for the best that I can't see what he's doing until he leaps and suddenly we're flying out the window. "—it!" I finish in a high warbling scream.

Did I say flying?

We fall. Like rocks. Two carefully entwined rocks— one of which was scrambling desperately to grab a tighter hold on the other right before he executed the most ludicrous superhero landing on the hood of someone's pickup truck.

Startled shouts yelp out from those gathered on balconies all around the apartment complex.

Mine is among them.

So is, "*Pendejo!* My car, man!"

Leaping from the hood, Aleron runs to his car. My back and butt hit the passenger seat before I knew he had the door open.

"Buckle up," he says calmly, his blurring race around to the driver's side making it seem as if he just materialized like magic behind the steering wheel.

The vampire from Ms. Menendez's kitchen lies on the sidewalk, floundering weakly, his now crooked back obviously broken.

I grab for the seatbelt as all four tires squeal against the pavement. Aleron leaves eight feet of blackened rubber in his flight from Saguaro Canyons. Looking back over my shoulder, the last I see of the place that has been my home for two years, is the shadow of that kindly old vampire standing at the broken window we just escaped through.

 erris

"Who the hell was that?" I ask in a small, shaky voice.

"I don't know," Aleron replies. He's stiff, his expression unreadable, and if he keeps driving like this, he's probably going to kill us both.

Staring wide-eyed out the front windshield, I hang on to the dash with one hand and the oh-shit handle with the other. And yet, every time I get the urge to remind him that I'm still very mortal, I remember Ms. Menendez. That old woman was in everyone's business. She was grumpy and gossipy, and she often acted like she was mother over the entire apartment complex, but she didn't deserve to die like that.

Nobody does.

I'm responsible. Tears sting my eyes as I try to figure

out what I've done that could possibly explain all of this. "They killed everybody on my floor."

Glancing over his shoulder, Aleron switches lanes. "Far more likely, he killed everyone in your building."

That did not make me feel better. "He was waiting for me."

"Yes."

"Why was he waiting for me? How did he know Jez?"

"I don't know." His hands flex on the steering wheel. "But I intend to find out."

That's when it strikes me just how odd it is for him to say such a thing. I look at him, scared and baffled. "Why? Why are you trying to involve yourself any deeper in this, with me? You could have been killed back there too."

His scoff is little more than breath. "An infant may choose to wrestle a cougar, but which do you think will come out the winner?"

"Yeah, but *who's* the cougar?"

He gives me a side-eyed glance. "I will pull this car over, darling Merris. Don't test me."

We're doing at least double the speed limit and sometimes faster. We run stop signs and stop lights, and he must have the kind of luck that inspires lottery ticket purchases, because we don't pass a single cop. Pedestrians get out of our way. So do the other drivers on the road, and those who don't, he swerves around. Aleron must be doing something, I'm certain of it, but unlike when he crawls into my head, I can't feel anything. Only the cold, sickly knots still tightening in my stomach and chest until it feels as if I can't breathe at all.

"Calm yourself," Aleron says.

I'm trying. I really am, but this is crazy. This isn't normal at all, and I don't just mean his driving. What the hell has happened to the world as I thought I knew it? A month ago, everything was fine. Now, my sister is gone and vampires don't just exist, they want me dead.

I shake my head, but no matter how hard I try, I can't make sense of it. "Why me? What have I done? I don't understand."

"Neither do I," says the vampire beside me. "Do you feel up to finding out?"

I don't have a choice. "How?"

He doesn't look at me, but weaves seamlessly into the gap that two slowing cars create beside us so he can take the onramp onto I-10. "We're going to ask someone to undo a mistake I made."

"Who?" I ask. "What mistake?"

Again, I get a side-eyed look.

"Do you remember last night at the club when I saved your life?"

It's hard not to feel a sting at that. "You think helping me was a mistake?"

Of course, he does. Tonight, it almost got him killed. Again.

"No, what I did before that was."

Now that we're on the interstate, he's not slowing down. The flattening effects of gravity meld me to the chair as he takes the car faster than I have ever been in a vehicle. Honestly, I'm not an adventurous soul and that isn't saying much. But it's definitely a shock to glance over and see 215 on the digital speedometer.

"Can we please slow down?"

"No." Aleron moves into the fast lane. "We are far from safe and the more time that passes, the less safe we're going to be."

I am in so far over my head, I don't know how to do anything more than put myself completely in this man's hands. It's at once the scariest and the most comforting thing I can think of. How can it not be? He's saved my life twice now. Even if he does regret it.

"There are certain rules, my darling Merris, that simply cannot be broken."

"What rules? What are you talking about?"

"You," he says pointedly, giving me another look.

I'm lost. Rattled as I am, none of this is making sense.

"Vampires," he all but snaps, exasperated. "We live among humans, and we can do so peacefully only for so long as the mortal half do not know about it."

"You mean the edible half?"

"It is a harmless arrangement..."

"Harmless?" I bark incredulously. "Try telling that to all those people—" Those dead people... because of me. I could cry.

"That was an anomaly."

"Anomaly my ass! They were *people*! People I knew!"

"I meant, most of us go through great effort to make sure it doesn't happen like that. Not anymore."

There are certain times when meant, intent and effort count for shit, and this is one of them. "Bullshit. Because it happened like that tonight."

I twist in my seat, putting my back to him as much as possible with the seatbelt still on and the graze on my ribs aching. We drive in silence so heavy I feel crushed by it.

"Are you menstruating?" he eventually asks.

I jerk around far enough to glare at him. "Is that your way of saying I'm being an irrational bitch?"

I'm shaking. I can't remember another time when I've ever felt so dangerously angry.

He doesn't look at me. "You're bleeding."

The statement cuts through my anger, setting me adrift. I'm still shaking, but now all I feel is helpless.

I think I hate him.

Snapping back over to face the window again, I fold my arms tight across my chest. I hunch down in my seat as if I can somehow disappear into it. I want to cry, but though my eyes burn furiously, I can't even do that.

The world is passing so fast outside it's giving me a headache. I close my eyes, which only seems to make the burning worse.

Aleron doesn't speak again, but eventually he slows down and just before we reach the turnoff from I-10 to I-19, he pulls over on to the side of the freeway. It's not yet ten o'clock and the traffic, although not as heavy as during the day, isn't light. Still, Aleron only waits long enough for an eighteen-wheeler to go barreling past fast enough to rock the car, and then he gets out.

I lock the doors just before he reaches me.

He unlocks them—fucking key fob—and opens the door. Hunkering down beside me, he checks my ribs first, then my neck. When I feel his hand touch the hem of the man's button-down shirt I'm wearing—*his* shirt, damn it— I quickly grab the two halves, folding them over one another, and shove them down between my legs to block him.

Letting his hand rest on my thigh, he studies me. Ours is a silent battle of wills, and one that I inevitably lose. I move my hands, but only because I know he can just compel me to anyway.

He checks me… down there. All I can do is sit, blushing, helplessly angry, and trying not to react to the near-impersonal touch of his fingers. They come away only slightly damp, but not with blood.

Finally, he finds it, a scratch on the back side of my left thigh where I must have got cut when we went out the window. It isn't deep, but I must have pulled it open again when I twisted sideways on the seat. From the inner pocket of his suit jacket, he pulls out a white handkerchief, which he uses to stop the bleeding again. One of the benefits to riding along with a vampire with impeccable fashion sense —there's always a handkerchief when you need one.

Abandoning his hanky to its new role in life as my bandage, Aleron stands up.

"Why are you doing this?" I can't help but ask.

He looks at me for a long time in silence, picking through a veritable minefield of answers before giving me none of them. His mouth opens, but then closes again without a word. Closing the door instead, he gets back in the car and quickly merges us back into traffic.

I face the window with my eyes closed against the burning, the heavy silence only getting heavier with every mile.

I wonder what it was he thought better of saying to me.

I wonder even more why it matters.

~

Aleron

WHY ARE YOU DOING THIS? she asks.

I almost tell her, but manage to stop myself in time. The answer could not be more obvious or more wrong, and I am made very uncomfortable by it.

Because she's mine.

Because I would no sooner abandon her to die than I would willingly walk out into the bright burning light of the sun.

I've never felt this before. When I was human, the middle son of a noble lord, I was quite handy with the ladies. My prey then consisted of the servants and what daughters and wives could be enticed from among the serfs who owed my father their tithe and their loyalty. I grew fond of some. One I even professed to love, but in all the years since, I have come to learn that I was far too self-absorbed and interested in my own pleasure to love anyone else.

Then came the call of the crusades and—for the promise of money, land, a title of my own, not to mention the succubus allure of what promised to be a grand adven-ture, I answered.

In the Muslim-controlled city of Antioch, I found my death at the hands of a vampire who wanted only to be left alone. He made me. He made others as well. We became Antioch's thirstiest army, feeding unfettered on soldiers from both sides, and what did I fall in love with then, but the intoxication of life everlasting. The unparalleled rush that comes of filling my sluggish veins with the rich euphoria emptied from another's.

I suppose that is love of a sort, but it doesn't last.

Eventually, we turned on each other, animals that we were.

I am the last of my nest and somewhere in the long line of centuries that have passed between then and now, I have evolved. The selfishness of the nobleman is gone. So is the warrior, turned blood-thirsty killer. I read books now. I have learned how to feed without killing. I have learned how to be sociable in the company of others. I have learned how to be civilized.

And jaded.

And bored.

But this... this unbearable fondness... somehow it has worked its way into me. It crouches in my chest where a beating heart ought to be, and the roots of it burrow in far beyond my ability to pluck them out again.

This is not a mess of my making. I don't know who made this mess, but I do know I won't abandon Merris to face it alone.

Because she's mine, though she shouldn't be. It took nine centuries for me to find this, and yet it is no kindness for her.

I want her with the same unbearableness that makes a newly-sired ache to feed.

I want her that badly, but I can't have her. I shouldn't.

I won't.

I'll get her through this, but as soon as I can make her safe, I am going to wipe her mind. I'll rob her of every trace of me, and then I'll melt back into the shadows. I'll keep watch, just to make sure she stays safe and that she never needs for anything. Eventually, she'll fall in love with another. She'll marry, have babies, grandbabies. She'll grow old where I can't. She'll die, leaving me behind.

Life as it should be.

I miss her already.

The Tohono O'odham exit comes up, and her head lifts off the pillow of her headrest when I take it.

"Where are we going?" she asks.

"San Xavier del Bac Mission," I tell her, even as we pass the sign giving directions to the old church.

"Why?" she asks, and I can hear it in her voice. She doesn't know why we're here, but she's pretty sure it's not because I've suddenly found God or an urge to pray.

"I need to ask a question, and he's the only one I know who might have the answer."

"He?" She sits up a little straighter, watching out the front windshield as the lights of the mission come into view. "He who?"

"Ignacio Gaona," I tell her.

"A vampire," she guesses. "Who lives in a church?"

"He doesn't just live here," I don't bother to hide my amusement at her dubious tone. "Once upon a time, he helped rebuild this place after it was destroyed in an Apache attack. Let's hope he's still in residence."

She stares at the welcome sign as we pass it, and probably at the mission's visiting hours clearly posted at the bottom. The last tourists were sent home hours ago. Apart from my car, pulling up to one of the front stalls, the parking lot is empty.

"We are so getting arrested," she says, shouldering open the door.

"Oh ye of little faith," I say dryly, unsure if I ought to be amused or insulted that she thinks I would ever allow myself to get arrested.

It's all right. She's still learning. I'll forgive her.

I also take the lead, carrying her upon my back because she has no shoes and really, what is Arizona but one gigantic cactus needle puncture waiting to happen? With her arms wrapped around my neck and her legs around my hips, I wend my way around one of the state's oldest churches, through the garden to the stone hill that rises out of the desert landscape. The simple cross atop it is illuminated, but the rest is dark, including the stone grottos around the base, one of which houses a saintly statue with hands serenely splayed as if in adoration of all the flowers, candles and offerings that litter its base from both pilgrims and tourists alike.

I've never been here before, but I've heard about it. Like most vampires aged enough to know how to survive on our own, there are certain things that we just can't help keeping track of. Shifter packs are one, since a careless move into the wrong territory could easily get us killed. But also, vampires older and more powerful than ourselves, sometimes for the same reason.

That is how I know to reach into the shadows behind the statue, feeling along the craggy rocks for something that moves when you push it. I disturb a tarantula tucked within a long crack, but eventually I do find it.

When I push, a low grinding signals the opening of a hidden entryway in the next shadowy recess over. There are no lights and very quickly the shadows swallow what few steps I can see leading down into the dark. Activating the flashlight on my cellphone, I set Merris down safely upon the steps.

"Stay close," I command, and carefully start down this narrow flight of steps. The Arizona night is cool, but under the hill it's much cooler. The temperature doesn't affect me any more than the darkness, but Merris is another matter, and when the hidden doorway to the surface world slowly grinds closed again, her shivers tremble through the hand that suddenly grabs my arm. There is now nothing but blackness above and below us, with only a handful of steps illuminated in what should have been the brightness of my phone. Quiet, cool, still as a tomb, it's as if the black of the stones swallow the light.

"Please tell me we're not now stuck down here," she says, staring up into the darkness.

"I'm almost certain I can find a way out," I reply. "I've never been here before, so it might take some time."

"Okay," she said, visibly struggling to be comforted.

"One night, maybe three or four at most."

She nods.

"It's all right," I add. "I brought a snack."

Nervous she might be, but she's not stupid. Catching herself mid-nod, she glares at me. "Ha ha," she deadpans.

Well, I thought it was funny.

Giving her my coat for warmth, we continue down.

The stairs are evidence that someone with an experienced and patient hand was long at work, building this place. There are no twists or curves, no widenings in the span. I turn almost sideways to keep my shoulders from brushing and possibly wedging between opposite rock walls. I'm tempted to think someone watches too many vampire movies, but these steps go on for far too long, taking us well below the surface and far, far from where I parked my car. This kind of care speaks to age and very old fears at what being discovered would mean.

Twice Merris stops. Leaning against the wall, she picks her feet up, cupping her toes in her hands to warm them. There is no room, or I would carry her to spare her from the cold of the rocks. The only thing I can do is give her my socks and shoes. She looks like a child playing dress up in Papa's clothes, clomping down the stone steps just behind me, one small hand on my shoulder to help keep her balance.

She is darling. That fondness for her helps distract me from the fact that I am now as undressed as I have ever been in public.

And then we come to the bottom, the last two steps of which open up wide enough for Merris and I to stand side-by-side, staring at the giant dead end before us. The stone slab that blocks our way is as smoothly chiseled as the ground beneath our feet. If there is another secret button or lever, I can't find it, though I spend considerable time searching. Merris holds the phone aloft while I feel my way along everything—the dead-end slab, both walls, the floor and even several steps up. Tall as I am, I can't reach the ceiling.

"What do we do now?" The stone eats her soft voice every bit as much as it devours the light. Barely an echo of it drifts back up the steps the way we've come.

"We wait." Giving my trousers a tug, I lower myself to

sit on the third step from the bottom. "Come," I offer her both my hand and my lap so she will not have to sit on the chilly stairs, and she accepts.

All my years of civility culminate in very little from the moment she crawls onto my lap. Her back to my chest, the heat of her body seeps into me. I'm not much better than the cold stone all around us, but I do my best to keep her warm. Taking off my shirt, I use it as a blanket for her legs, tucking the ends in around her icy feet and even rubbing her toes. My shoes were too big to stay on her feet, and I could feel how cold they are through the thin weave of my socks.

I really will be naked by the time I get out of here.

"Thanks," she says softly, hugging herself as she curls into me.

"Of course," I reply, like a gentleman instead of one headily aware of the heat emanating from her sex and bottom. I both feel, hear, and smell the pulse of her beating heart. Her hair tickles my cheek when she bows her head, looking at my phone still clasped in her small hand.

"How old are you?" she asks. "Have you seen many things?"

"Many," I assure her, happily granting both our needs for distraction. "I was human when first I ventured off, against my father's wishes, mind you, to see how much wealth and adventure I could find on the crusades. I was as I am now when it came time for me to return, although it would be more than a hundred years before I chose to."

"Why?" She lays her head upon my shoulder like a child settling in for a story.

I can't help but stroke her soft hair, the dark strands

like the finest silk between my fingers. "I didn't want to watch my family succumb to age."

"Have you traveled?" she asks around a soft yawn.

"Oh yes. Let me see." What stories can I tell her that don't involve death and feeding? "Europe, Africa, the Orient back when it was called such."

"And now you live in Arizona, and you're a member of an S&M club where people go to get snacked on."

A smile tugs my tips. "Only the lucky ones."

"How is that lucky?"

In the light of my cellphone, I show her my right hand. "I could make you come, Merris my darling, with nothing more than my smallest finger. Would you like me to show you?"

She squirms, her hot bottom grinding against my lap. "That's okay," she demurs, looking away so I won't see her blushing.

"Are you sure?" I love teasing her. Her blush deepens, but her tell-tale heart quickens and the heat between her thighs grows beautifully scented.

I stroke her hair again, before letting my left hand steal up under the silken tresses to cup the back of her neck. I caress her, gentle up and down strokes of my thumb following her spine. Have her nipples pebbled into nibble-able peaks yet? Swaddled as she is in my coat, it's impossible to tell, but I would bet so. I am arousing her.

She doesn't say no, either. She doesn't say anything, and when she shivers again, I know it's not solely because of the cold.

"How often do you go?" she asks, her normally soft voice slightly husky.

"Club Toxic?" When she nods, I slip my fingers up her neck, combing them up into the soft hair to caress her scalp. "Often."

"Did…" Her breath catches slightly. "Did we have sex there?"

My hand stills in her hair. "No," I answer, unsure if I ought to be surprised or appalled that my mind wipe seems not to have been as successful as I thought. "What do you remember?"

"My wrists cuffed to a bar, hoisted above my head."

My eyebrows arch.

"You're standing behind me." Hesitantly, she looks at me. "Your arms are around me. You're kissing my neck as you reach down between my legs with that glove on your hand, and then you…" She flushes even brighter, her traitorous little heart beating faster. "You're… sliding into me… from behind."

"That was not at all what happened," I tell her, beyond surprised. "Mind you, I'm far from opposed, but this is what your memories tell you?"

I often make suggestions when I wipe thoughts, but I don't know any vampire who can replace true memories with fictional ones.

Staring into my eyes, a flicker of uncertainty creeps into hers. "Did you do that to my sister?"

"No." Firmly and I hope for the last time, I tell her, "I did nothing but offer Jez a ride home the night she died. She refused. I regret that I did not insist. Answer me now, this is what your memories tell you I did?"

Very slightly, she shakes her head. "It's what I see in my dreams," she reluctantly confesses. "I've seen your face every night for weeks now. I saw it the night she died. At first, I thought it was you doing that to her, but then that guy at the club grabbed my arm—"

"The one I slammed against the wall?"

She nods. "And now, all I see is you and me and strange sex in strange places. Like at your house, in your bathroom."

"One would think I'd pick a more romantic, if not sanitary location." I can hardly think.

"I think I was seeing what we did in the bedroom. I got the wallpaper by the door wrong."

"I swear the contractor bought every roll of that godawful pattern that he could find. It's in every room of the house." I really must be besotted because, despite the incredulous nature of her claim, I find myself inclined to believe her.

"We're about to lose the light," she says.

And I'll be damned, but no sooner does my gaze drop to my phone than does it wink out, casting us abruptly into pitch dark.

"Dear God." The sound of my surprise echoes in the inky black. "You're psychic."

And she has seen us in entwined intimately together, not once but multiple times. That is not like me. That is more than just feeding. It's more than mere fondness or my besotted allure to someone who should have been nothing more than supper.

"Well," she hedges, "yes. Although to be fair, your phone's been on two-percent power for a while now."

Dear God. Beautiful, quick-witted, smart, *and psychic*. I think I love this girl.

CHAPTER 10

A leron

"We're going to die down here," Merris says in the dark.

"No, we're not," I promise, still the chair on which she sits to protect her from the leeching cold of the stone steps. Now and then, I feel her shivering. The longer we sit here, the worse that is going to get. I have to find a way to get us out, but without light by which to see, my chances of finding something diminishes while her risk of hypothermia grows, starting the minute I put her down.

"We are," she insisted. "One of us absolutely is."

"Merris…"

"One of us brought a snack, the other brought a vampire," she snips. "Tell me, how long can you go without eating before you snap and rip my—"

Catching a fistful of hair at the back of her head, I yank her head back and silence her the best way I can. Kissing her is surprisingly pleasant for me. I rarely find it so. Intimacy has always been a tool for me. Something I can use to get close to my prey. A kiss upon warm lips to sharpen my senses while lulling their own. A finger beneath the chin to tilt the head back, while a short, seductive nibble along the neck takes me to the pulse that draws me most.

I can count on two hands the number of partners with whom I have done more than kiss, and still have fingers left over. None were love matches, although my kind are prone to them. Look at Lucius, Tucson's very own vampire King—at least among his sizeable if slightly less than devoted nest. He not only mated, but—and quite infamously so—he mated a shifter. I have seen her, from a distance. A lovely, pale-pelted creature. I sincerely doubt theirs is a platonic relationship.

Many among my kind are, however. We drift through the centuries together, isolating ourselves among the food supply as a means of survival, meeting in public only while hunting and only if it can't be avoided. We smile and we chit-chat, all while masking our grave mistrust of one another until something brings that mistrust to the surface, and then somebody usually dies.

Few matings last forever. In my experience, intellectual bonds are almost always stronger than sexual ones, and yet this feels so very much different from anything I have known before. Her lips are different, soft, supple, yielding beneath my own. The ties of her hair wrapping my fingers hold me every bit as captive as I hold her, drinking in the sigh she exhales as I coax her lips to part.

I want inside of her.

I want to wrap myself in the heat of her eager limbs,

feeling the arching, writhing, undulations of her body as my hips rock within the cradle of hers. I want to feel the beat of her racing heart while my chest is pressed to hers, and my hand holds her throat, and my lips and tongue flick and tease and mate with her own, and the spasms of her tight flesh convulse around my cock until we are both too exhausted by it to move one thrust more.

I lift my lips from hers, all but drunk on my own wanting of her.

"—my throat out," she stubbornly finishes, as if I'd never kissed her at all.

I tsk, but the urge to put her across my knee is tempered by the amusement she sparks. "I'm not going to hurt you."

"You'll be crazed. You won't even know you're doing it."

"I think someone has seen too many horror movies. Do you need to be put on television restriction when we get back to the surface world?"

My grip on the back of her head lets me feel the glare she casts my way. "Like you could ever stop me from doing something if I really wanted to do it."

"Be careful when issuing challenges you'd rather I not accept."

Her body is absolutely still on my lap. "I wasn't issuing challenges."

I don't bother answering. We both know she was.

Her little bottom squirms. "All right," she says, her tone painstakingly neutral despite the very faintest tremble of unease. I've pricked her curiosity. I can tell by the quickening in her pulse that she isn't altogether put off by the idea of being constrained by a few of my rules. "How?"

She rolls her shoulders, shifting as my thumb strokes the side of her neck.

"How, what?"

"How would you stop me? What would you do?"

"Are you seriously asking a vampire you know to be a sadist at an S&M club how he'd choose to curtail you?"

"How do I know you're a sadist?" she shoots back. "You could be a freaky masochist who likes being tied down and tickled with ostrich feathers."

I truly am falling in love with her. Her mouth, on the other hand, is about to get her spanked. "No offense, darling, but there is nothing in this world that could ever tempt me to let anyone tie me down."

"Why not?"

The darkness completely invalidates the incredulous look I give her. "Sadist," I repeat, hoping my tone will convey how obvious this should be.

"Yeah, but are you really? Or do you just like making people bleed because it's akin to ringing the dinner bell? I don't think you're sadistic at all. Otherwise, why haven't you hurt me?"

"It didn't hurt when I bit your clit?"

"Feeding," she says, completely discounting it.

As much as I would dearly love to point out the scene we played out in Club Toxic's dungeon, unfortunately she won't remember it, and I don't want to have the whole 'what do you mean you wiped my memories' argument with her right now.

"See?" she says, as my silence stretches on. "While I

don't doubt for a second that some vampires are sadists, or that you might have done sadistic things in the past, I really don't think you yourself are a sadist at your core."

"Oh, darling, you really have no idea."

"You're sitting here half-naked on the stairs while I'm on your lap comfortably burritoed in your clothes so I don't have to be cold. Those are not the actions of a hard-core sadist."

"How would you know?"

"I read de Sade over summer vacation for extra credit in high school. It was the biggest collective works book I could find, and I wanted to shock the shit out of my English teacher."

"And did you learn anything?"

"Apart from his being twisted and gross, nothing of any interest. You didn't even tie me up before you bit me."

"I left you chained to my bed all day long."

"Yes, but only so I wouldn't escape. If one can discount the thorns, your bed was very soft and you were careful to provide me with food and water, and easy access to the bathroom so I wouldn't be uncomfortable. You haven't whipped me. You haven't even spanked me. In fact, every time I get hurt, you take care of me. Does that sound like the actions of a sadis—"

I flip her over my lap so fast all she had time to do is yelp before the flat of my hand finds her shapely ass in the darkness, delivering a flurry of brisk slaps meant to put an end to this ridiculous discussion. I give her only a dozen or so swats, but each one is delivered with a firm arm and she takes them all with little more than shrill gasps and squeaks that echo up the stone steps along with each crack of impact. Then, righting her once more, I calmly straighten my coat about her shoulders and adjust the now disheveled shirt over her lap, tucking it in around her legs and feet to keep her from the cold.

In my calmest tone, I ask, "Are we finished?"

She holds herself quiet and still upon my lap for a full count of three before shrugging her arm out of my coat. Sticking it down between us, every slumbering nerve in my body snaps to wakefulness when she cups the front of my trousers, adjusting her palm upon the full length of my cock. The heat of her tiny fingertips scalds through cloth straight into my balls. The palm of her hand is the most delicious fire.

"Not hard in the slightest," she decides, taking back her hand with a sniff and settling into my coat once more. "Definitely *not* a sadist."

I can't move, I dare not. It takes every ounce of control I have not to throw her down right here on these stairs and show her just how hard I am fast becoming, with her touch echoing through my flesh and the heat of her well-smacked ass burning my thighs. I should pick her up and move her off my lap, deposit her on the stairs, move myself as far from her as I can get in the confines of this place, but I won't. I can't. There is a vampire on the other side of this door. I'm not about to leave her undefended in the darkness and for no other reason than because my cock feels like misbehaving.

On the other hand, she's awakened the beast. She can damn well attend it.

My arm hooks her waist, pulling her back up against my chest, and my hand catches her throat, silencing whatever protest she would otherwise give before she can do more than draw the breath for it. The heady thump of her pulse teases my fingertips as I draw her back against me. She stiffens, trying not to resist, but my gentle insistence wins her over. Reluctantly, she relaxes against me, laying her head back on my shoulder as I wish it. I reward her submission with a kiss to that soft, sweet place right behind her ear.

I feel her nervous swallow against my hand as I continue to hold her throat and, with my other, I undress her, pulling my coat off her shoulders but leaving her hands bound within its sleeves.

"Do not move unless I move you," I murmur behind her ear. "Do not speak unless I allow it. If you wish to stop, your safeword is Rumpelstiltskin. If you cannot speak, tap my hand, do you understand?"

She barely nods.

"Out loud, please," I remind her, tightening my arm around her waist and pulling her back on my lap until she is forced to straddle my thighs. Her back to my chest, her head tipped to rest on my shoulder, I have the heat of her ass right where I want it. Can she feel how hard I am now? All that I am is hardness, pressed to all the softest parts of her.

"Yes," she whispers.

Gently, I nip her ear, letting her feel the tips of my teeth. "Yes, what?" I remind her, silkenly.

Her involuntary squirm could have made a saint come, but it's not a saint's lap she's sitting on.

"M-Master," she stammers.

Good girl.

Undressing her is like unwrapping a present I cannot see. But while the dark might rob my eyes of this experience, my other senses exalt. I bare her to the cold one button at a time until the two halves of my shirt fall open. Peeling the cloth off her shoulders, I leave her arms bound in the sleeves here too and my shirt and coat both puddled around her waist like a forgotten wrap.

My fingers read her goosebumps like braille on the pages of her body—up the side of her arm, across her chest where the soft flesh of her breasts rise and fall as she breathes—it tells a story. So do her shivers as I explore her, the naked swells of her breasts with the buds of her nipples tightening beneath each passing caress of my fingertips, the flinching softness of her belly as I caress downward and pull away the cloth that covers her lap.

She shakes, but this is more than just cold. It's me she shakes for, and I enjoy every intensifying quiver as I part her legs with little more than a touch to each thigh.

"Wider," I tell her, returning my hand to the flat of her stomach.

Her breath catching, she opens her legs wide.

Her whole body stiffens when I taste her, flicking the pulse on the side of her neck with my tongue before gracing it with a kiss. Her muscles lock as I open my mouth, but I don't bite. I suckle and I lay claim, but I don't feed, and with each pull of my mouth, the tension seeps from her. Hers is a shaky, reluctant sigh as she relaxes against me again.

Right until my hand on her throat tightens and I cut off her air. A few seconds only. Just enough for her to notice, and tense again. Immediately I let her breathe and as she sweeps in that latent gasp, I lay my claim between her legs next.

Her clit will be tender for days yet. I know it's my teeth she's feeling there too as I part her folds with my fingers, releasing her scent into the air and allowing the cold to take its most illicit kiss of the wetness I've found.

Her hips twitch, the tiniest buck up into my caressing hand as I dip my fingers in all that slick, feminine heat and spread the moisture all over the bud of her swollen clit. She's fighting herself to hold still—fighting and failing, her luscious body arching as she stifles a moan. Her ass grinds against the bulge of my cock, and I know she definitely feels my hardness now because she's shifting her hips in an effort to direct how it touches her.

"Naughty girl. Didn't I tell you don't move?" I cut off her air again, my other hand caressing her clit in fast, circular strokes. Her hips buck, her heels smacking against a stone step as her whole body tightens.

Again, I relax my hold on her throat after only a few seconds. The caresses continue, quick circles against the very tender tip of her clit until the echoes of her wetness in the dark can be heard right alongside her soft, moaning breaths. Her legs shake all around mine. Her bottom clenches, alternately bucking up into my rapidly stroking hand and cringing back against my captive cock.

I never have been one to tolerate being held against my will.

With a brisk slap to her eager pussy, I let her go long enough to free myself from my trousers. The heat of her ass is the closest thing to heaven I will ever know, and I quickly hook her waist again, lifting her high. Hard as I am, my cock springs forward, the tip sliding into wetness the instant I lower her again.

She moans, her thighs shaking and her ass grinding the whole way down. The twitchy spasms of her muscles lock down on me. Those spasms go wild when my grip on her throat tightens again. She tries to ride me. I rub, teasing her, my fingers on her clit never still and always changing sensation, pinching, caressing, spanking, tickling just to feel her writhing with such abandon, and she is only getting wetter.

I wish I could see her.

Her heartbeat is a frantic drumming that pounds in my senses. I hear it, feel it beneath my fingers, around my cock, beneath my lips as I kiss and suckle that seductive jugular vein on the side of her neck. I've never wanted to bite anyone as badly as I do right now, but I don't. It's too soon for her.

I want to thrust, to bury myself deep inside her enchanting heat. Neither is going to happen in this position, but baring her to the cold of the air is nothing compared to laying her down in a rock cave. I won't do that.

So, I deny myself, just like I deny her, cutting her air off again and again. Denial can be exquisite torment. Hers is edging her to completion, teasing her with the raw fury of all that pent-in sensation, allowing her only quick, gasping sips as I change sensations again. Now, I give her the swift, circular clit strokes designed to make her come, but only while I'm choking her. The minute I let go, my other hand stops.

Her shaky gasps become ragged moans, tinged with

frustration. She's trying to choke herself now, catching and holding her breath so I'll squeeze my fingers and edge her closer still. She grinds, rocks, fights to bounce in what few inches of movement I'll allow her while I tickle her pretty clit and listen to the beating of her heart.

I know when she's ready. One last release of her neck to let her catch her breath, but this time my fingers between her clenching thighs do not go still.

I want to bite so badly.

Shutting off her air, I make her come instead. She arches, back bowing, muscles both quaking and straining, convulsing with the shivery spasms that dance along my cock. I take her right to the edge of passing out before I release her throat for the very last time. She's gasping, choking, whimpering ragged sobs that might yet tip over that edge into honest tears of release when, suddenly, there's a click and the stone slab blocking our way rumbles into motion.

Light floods the stairwell, blocked by the shadow of a tall, lean man wearing jeans, of all things, and a soft gray sweater. His long brown hair hangs straight to his collar. His narrow face catches the shadows until it seems as if the darkness has cut him into angles.

Hands braced to either side of the doorway, he growls, "When I don't open my door right away, most people get the not-so-subtle hint, and they go away. What they do *not* do is bang one another on my steps, leaving bodily fluids all over the damn place." Shoving backwards off the wall, he shakes his head in disgust. "Rude," he says, and walks away.

Merris

I'VE NEVER BEEN in a tomb before. I don't know if this actually is one, but Ignacio—Aleron's very grumpy friend —has carved himself out one hell of a catacomb. Catacomb? More like honeycomb, with bare bulb lights strung on extension cords across the roundish cavern that makes up his den and shadows that drip like black honey down the walls and across the floor, flowing into box-like crevices that notch the vertical bedrock everywhere there's room enough to make one. All of them are stuffed quite full of books. New books, old books, books without covers and bindings tied with string, scrolls, maps, folded bit of parchments—and all of it is layered in dust.

"The maid service is a little slow here," Ignacio says coolly when I'm not quite as secretive as perhaps I should be, running my finger through the thick layer at the mouth of one stone cubbyhole.

"Where did you get all this?" I breathe, half in wonder, half appalled. As much as I love to read, I've never seen anything like this. The smell is quite musty, making me sneeze each time I lean close enough to try to read. Not every tome has writing on the cover or even enough of a cover left to protect the pages. What words I can make out are rarely written in English. "Have you read them?"

"Of course, I have." Thoroughly irritated, Ignacio looks from me to Aleron. "Knowledge is power, young lady. There are billions upon billions of words written on these pages. What good does it do if no one reads them? I swear," he says, shooting Aleron an accusing stare, "we're hardly better than monkeys. What do you want?"

"Information," Aleron replies. "A piece of a puzzle you hopefully know."

Spreading his hand, the other vampire indicates the whole of his honeycomb of books and waits.

"A vampire lord has moved his nest into the Tucson area and I want to know who he is."

"You're going to have to be a touch more specific than that," Ignacio says dryly. "Although not as plentiful as the written word, we do tend to be prolific when we get lonely."

"I believe he's an old soul and powerful. We ran into him earlier tonight. He not only masked his presence from me, he masked all but the one meant to draw my attention."

"An uncommon ability," Ignacio acknowledges. "But not unheard of."

"He was an old man when he was sired."

Why that should make a difference, I don't know, but the other vampire's attention abruptly intensifies.

"Full head of gray hair or bald on top with no more than a sprig around his pate, like a Roman emperor's laurel leaf crown?"

"Definitely the crown," Aleron replied.

"How old?"

"Fifty at least when he was turned."

I've spent too much time with Aleron, I think. I see the subtle shift in Ignacio's expression—the flattening of his mouth, the faint quirk of a brow—just before he turns away. He fetches a book, an old one almost two feet in length, thick and heavy. Its leather-bound cover is chipped and peeling, and its unevenly cut pages are yellowed with age and worn around the edges.

Laying it on a stack of more books on a cluttered table, he opens it carefully. Each page is blank, but between the sheaves are other pages—drawings, wanted posters, newspaper articles. He stops at a drawing, studies it silently a moment, and then steps back for Aleron to take a closer look.

"That's him," Aleron says softly. "Who is he?"

"At one time, he was known as Athanasius. I believe he goes by Arthur now." Ignacio frowns. "He's hunting you?"

"No." When Aleron looks at me, so too does the other vampire.

He blinks, all traces of irritation melting into surprise as he glances at Aleron again. "Why?"

"I was hoping you could tell me."

Tipping his head, Ignacio blinks again. "I do not have a crystal ball, young man. How exactly do you think I'm supposed to do that?"

"They say you can read the mind of any vampire who comes within a mile of you. It's why you live so far underground. To get away from the constant chatter."

Ignacio frowns, and Aleron asks, "How good are you with humans?"

"Wait a minute." I step back, not at all liking the way the two of them are suddenly looking at me. "What exactly are you trying to do?"

Bowing his head, Aleron looks away from me. If I

didn't know better, I'd think it a guilty reaction, but it makes no sense.

"I already told you," I say. "I've never met this Arthur... Athanasius... whoever he is. I don't know why he's after me. What possible use could it do to read my mind?"

"There's nothing in there to read," Ignacio snaps irritably. "Also, it looks like a guilty reaction because that's exactly what it is. He likes fucking you and doesn't want to have to admit he wiped your memories the other night. And no," he says, turning back to Aleron, "I can't undo the damage. Our kind does not simply crawl in and out of human heads without risk. What you're asking me to do might just as easily leave her simple and drooling on herself, so let me save you the trouble. Athanasius is a leech. He moves his nest from place to place, continent to continent, never staying anywhere for longer than a few months, because he can't. He's never been careful where he feeds. He doesn't care how many bodies he leaves in his wake. He doesn't want your meat bag either, he could care less about sweetening the blood. He moved beyond that centuries ago."

"What do you mean, moved beyond that?" Aleron frowns.

Myself, I'm still floundering much further back in the conversation. "What do you mean, wiped my memories?"

Ignacio gives us identical withering stares. "He wiped your memories," he tells me, "because humans are panicky animals who react badly to knowing they aren't at the top of the food chain. And Athanasius doesn't give two shits for this girl," he tells Aleron, "because the only thing he cares about is getting high. He was sucking *nepenthes* from Egyptian royalty three thousand years before the illegitimate son of a carpenter kicked the Roman hornets' nest, and he's still supping it—albeit now as heroin—from the veins of whoever he can enthrall off the dance floor at Lucius's nightclub. He doesn't *care* if you know about it," he spits at me, and then to Aleron says, "He doesn't care if *you* know it either. The only one he can't afford to have knowledge of it is Lucius, at least not until he finagles a strong enough foothold on that vampire king's hunting ground to snatch it out from under him."

"Lucius will never let that happen," Aleron says.

"Lucius is distracted," Ignacio corrects. "He has a pretty she-wolf in his bed, his sired are ambitious and restless, and Athanasius *knows* it. He wants what Lucius has—a stable feeding ground close enough to the border where the drug supply is as endless as are the veins from which to drink it. It is also the one thing he will never be able to keep no matter how many times he keeps trying, because he's stupid, stoned and too reckless to maintain patience for any length of time. That's it. That's it in a nutshell. He wants Club Toxic."

"Then we go to Lucius," Aleron says, decided. "Let's see what he has to say about another king ousting him from his territory."

Ignacio snorts. "He might not be as much help as you think."

"You mean apart from the fact that shifters run Tucson, and they're far more likely to shut him down than we are? Yes." Aleron snorts now too. "I thought about that. But I don't happen to be on friendly terms with any, and I'd just as soon not have to ask one for help."

"Not that," Ignacio says, and there's a strangeness to his soft voice that catches even my attention.

All this time, I've been standing here, shocked to my core, searching my mind for a hollow in what I remember happening at the nightclub. I remember standing in line, being chosen to go inside, getting my drink, walking the perimeter of the dance floor, deciding to go home and then getting shot at. Somewhere in all that, I had a run-in with Aleron that he wiped away?

"Shit," Aleron says.

My attention comes back to them, but they aren't looking at me. They're looking up over the top of me. I look up too. There are eight big-screen TVs hanging suspended on the wall directly above my head, that I haven't noticed until now. Because of the way the ceiling juts in levels like stairs, it's not until I come all the way into the center of the room that I see them. They're on mute, with close caption text running along the bottom. All are turned to a different channel. One is streaming *The Great British Baking Show*. The rest are flashing pictures on the news. Three of those pictures are photos of me.

Finding the remote, Ignacio activates the sound on one in time for us all to hear a female newscaster saying, "… wanted for questioning in connection to the mass murder that happened tonight at Saguaro Canyons apartment complex. To recap, forty-one people were found slain in their homes at a complex where Miss Chapman also lived. No speculation can yet be made on what exactly happened, or why, but police…"

The television mutes again, leaving all of us standing in silence. I can't breathe. My chest is aching, suddenly so tight it's as if someone just reached in under my ribcage and grabbed me by the heart.

"They think I did that?" I choke.

"That's the magic of television," Ignacio muses. "Now everyone knows you did. They know your face, your name... What few friends you have who would never believe this of you, not in a million years, they won't matter. Because the only thing you can say in your own defense is the one thing no one will believe, and that's a vampire did it."

$\mathcal{M}$*erris*

I SIT on the steps just outside Ignacio's open door, still wearing the shirt Aleron gave me back at his house and his dress coat. Everything else, I've given back to him so he doesn't have to make the trek up to the surface world in nothing but his trousers. In my hands, I hold the socks Ignacio gave me, just before he shooed at me with both hands, said, "Go, house elf, you're free," and sent me out here.

He's an asshole too.

The socks are nice, though. They kind of look like homemade slipper socks, knitted in beige yarn on the outside, but with a thick lining of soft fake fur on the inside. I slip them on. The feet are a little big for me, but they're very warm. Wiggling my toes in softness, all I feel is hungry, tired and sad.

I'm pretty sure I'm going to prison for forty-one murders I didn't commit.

And that's only if I'm not horribly slaughtered by rogue vampires first.

I've no idea what a shifter is, but the world I thought I knew is suddenly a much bigger and scarier place than I ever imagined.

"I'd offer to let you hole up here for the next fifty years," Ignacio says as he escorts Aleron to the door. "But I don't think I like either of you that much. No offense."

"None taken," Aleron diplomatically replies. "Thank you for the flashlight."

"The button to get out is in the rocks above the door. Good luck," he says, withdrawing back into his room. "Please don't come back."

The heavy rock slab rumbles into motion, sliding with gravel grinding slowness until it's once more sealed and all the light is gone.

Shaking the flashlight until it comes on, Aleron offers me his hand but I shake it off. I'm still reeling from the mind-wipe revelation. Aleron is a vampire. *A vampire.* Capable of wiping entire memories from my mind. What did he wipe? How can I ever trust him again?

I can't. But unfortunately, I'm stuck with him for the moment, seeing as how the entire Tucson police force is looking for me and my sister's killer is still on the loose.

Up the stairs we go, single-file in most places because it's so narrow. I'm more than ready to be out of this hole by the time we reach the top. My legs are like rubber. I don't know how many times I had to stop and rest, but I've never felt so happy to see a car as I was once Aleron found the button releasing us back out into the night.

I slide into the passenger seat just as soon as he opens the door for me. "How much time do we have?" I ask, when he's sitting beside me. The whole car rumbles to life when he starts it.

"Not much," he says, one eye on the skyline which is already lightening to a plum-gray. "We have to hurry."

"Back to your house?"

"No. He saw me with you. My house won't be any safer than yours. The only thing working right now in our favor is the dawn. He can't hunt you in the day, unless he's using humans."

"You mean as more than a food source."

"It would make sense. Remember the man who grabbed your arm at the nightclub? He makes me wonder. A human could easily hunt other humans in that place without drawing too much scrutiny, and I hadn't seen Athanasius or any of his nest before tonight. It makes sense that he would have agents in Club Toxic who can pass under Lucius's radar."

"That's how he got to Jez." It hurt just to say it.

"Yes."

We drive in silence, speeding away from the mission, back up the freeway to Interstate 10, with the sky growing lighter by the second.

"If you want to crawl in the trunk, I can drive," I offer. That might be a lie, though. I've never driven a stick before.

The look he gives me pretty much kills that idea. "I am not crawling in the trunk." Glaring out at the road ahead, he adds, "You have no idea how to get where we're going anyway. And while I'll admit they're not going to be happy to see me, they sure as hell aren't going to let you in if I'm in the trunk. Chances are good they might not let us in no matter what we do."

"Who?" I ask.

"Lucius, king of his nest and, arguably, the most powerful vampire in Tucson." Aleron's hands on the steering wheel are tight. It might be a trick of my imagination because I know how important this is, but it feels as if we're driving even faster than he normally does.

"What's the plan if he doesn't let us in?" I'm almost afraid to ask.

"In all likelihood?" He glances at me sideways. "I will die and then so too, I suspect, will you. If not on Lucius's command, then certainly by Athanasius's once night falls again."

It doesn't take long to reach our destination. It must be a prerequisite—a person can't become a vampire unless they're rich. Or maybe this Lucius person simply isn't king for nothing. His house is huge. The yard lights are on and the gate that blocks the driveway is electronically locked.

Aleron looks at the speaker box for a long time before he glances at me, rolls his window down and presses the button. The horizon is scarily bright, the color of old bruises, with just a highlight of pink on the underside of distant clouds.

It's too close to dawn. I don't think anyone's going to answer. King or not, every vampire in that massive house has got to be tucked safely in their basement coffins by now. Jesus, am I about to watch Aleron go up in smoke and flames?

Panic sits in my chest like a cold fist, gradually tightening its grip with each irretrievable second that ticks on past us.

"We have to—" I forget what I'm about to say as the gate suddenly buzzes and opens, rattling back on its track and leaving the entire stretch of paved driveway open for us to approach. Not a single word comes from the speaker box. As Aleron puts the car into gear, the front porch light winks on and the door opens. No one steps out. "Yeah," I breathe. "This isn't ominous in the slightest."

I look to Aleron, but our misgivings don't change the facts. We're out of time and options.

Driving up to the house, we leave the car parked at the garage. I'm imagining all kinds of terrible things inside the darkness waiting for us beyond that open door. There isn't a single light on, and no one I can see is waiting to receive us.

Aleron takes the first step across the threshold, which startles me.

"Don't you need permission to enter?"

Tsking, he stops just shy of rolling his eyes. "You are definitely going on TV restriction. Besides, they opened the door specifically so we could come inside. That is permission."

Every curtain in the house is drawn, and once Aleron closes the door behind us, the only light we have is what slivers of a glow filter in through the cracks around the drapes that protect the porch windows. And then, suddenly, a light winks on further down the hall.

"This way," a woman calls.

"Kindly hurry," a man adds. "We haven't a lot of time."

I have more than a few misgivings, but when Aleron takes my arm, there's nothing I can do but follow in his footsteps. Down the hall, past the kitchen, living room, den, to a master bedroom where the giant king-sized bed lies folded up against the wall, revealing stone stairs leading down. A beautiful woman—tall, slender, her white-blonde hair flowing freely down her back—is waiting near the entryway. We've caught them in the process of going underground and neither seems happy to be sharing this secret with us.

And yet, she's the one who impatiently orders us to go down, waiting until we pass her before closing and locking the door behind us. We take the steep stairs down, following in the unhurried wake of a man even taller than Aleron.

The back of my neck prickles. I look back at the woman bringing up the rear of our very short train. Her stare is the coldest I think I've ever seen. She is not smiling. She is not friendly. She doesn't like me.

I face forward, holding on to Aleron's steadying arm with both hands now, all the way down into their sanctuary.

It's everything I imagine a vampire's lair would be. Like a crypt, the walls and floor are stone. I can smell the must of dry dirt, though I don't see bare earth anywhere. The floor is hard and cool, and we pass several small rooms before motion lights suddenly come on and we're standing in a large room decorated only with a large stone sarcophagus rising up out of the middle of the floor. The lid is slightly askew, revealing a coffin big enough for two, lined in soft velvet and pillows.

"I'm surprised she's not in bonds," the man I assume to be Lucius says, turning to face us now that we're all downstairs.

Releasing my hands, Aleron raises his hand to rest on the back of my neck. "Why would she be in bonds?"

"You are not here for the bounty?" Lucius asks. His face is a mask of politeness, but the air in here suddenly feels anything but. It's grown heavier, colder. Distinctly and silently hostile.

On the back of my neck, Aleron's fingers barely move, but I feel the tension in them. "What bounty?"

"The bounty I was forced to put up the minute I heard about the shifter slaughter at Saguaro Canyons. Now, the humans are blaming a human." Lucius looks at me and both the age and the cold of his stare bore into me. "But the problem is, one human did not kill the grand matriarch of the Camino Seco coyote pack, nor did the matriarch reek of vampire. So, I am going to ask this once. What happened at that apartment complex? And I promise if you lie to me, I won't bother ending either of you humanely. I'll just give you to the Camino Seco shifters."

"They won't end you humanely, either," the woman behind me growls.

"I don't believe this." I don't mean to sound as pathetic as I do, but the wounds are still too raw, and there's nothing so helpless and awful than not being able to prove your own innocence.

Worse than that, is this what the rest of my life is now

going to be? Everyone I knew is dead and everyone I met is going to look at me with this same cold anger on their faces.

"I just wanted to find out what happened to my sister. I didn't kill anyone!" I protest.

Unfazed, the woman steps in so close to me we are now toe-to-toe. "Prove it," she challenges.

I have no idea how.

"Give me your hands."

I glance at my hands, hesitating only a moment before offering them to her palm up. I don't know what I expected her to do. Hurt me, I think, but she doesn't, although I still jump when she clamps my wrists in her iron-like grip. She's slender, tall, beautiful, and strong as hell. She drags my hands up to her face, her gaze never once leaving mine. Not until her nose is right up against my fingertips. She breathes in, twice.

The cold anger in her face falters. Her eyebrows buckle as faint traces of moisture gather in her eyes. Releasing me, she abruptly backs away.

"Selene," Lucius says, holding out his arm for her.

She looks at me, and then to her mate, offering two shakes of her head before she turns from us all.

"I didn't do it," I say again, not understanding what's happening.

Catching my arm, Aleron pulls me out from between the other vampires. He tucks me behind him, but to me it already feels as if the danger has somehow passed. The woman's head is bowed, her shoulders slumped as if in defeat. She goes to Lucius, shaking her head. I can barely make out her voice as she whispers, "There's no trace of shifter on her."

"We won't stop looking until we find out what happened," the other vampire says, laying a comforting hand on her shoulder. "At this point, however, I think the explanation would serve everyone better if we wait to hear it until we've rested." Looking past her to Aleron and me, the vampire king hikes his chin to indicate behind us. "You can bed down in that room back there, if you like."

Regardless of how it's phrased, it's not an offer as much as it's a thinly veiled command. He doesn't trust us and, frankly, I'm not sure how much we can trust either of them. Not that we have any other option. By now, the sun is certainly up. We simply have no more time.

Aleron's hand at the small of my back nudges me into motion and back we go, into one of the adjacent rooms that looks more like cells now that I'm standing inside one. It sounds like one too when Lucius firmly shuts and locks us inside. There's even a small, barred window at face level in the heavy door, through which the vampire king says, "No offense."

"None taken," Aleron guardedly replies. "I wouldn't want strangers walking around while I sleep either."

"We will talk tonight," Lucius promises, and then he moves away, and I can't see or hear him anymore. I know he hasn't gone far and before more than a few minutes pass, I hear whispers. Then a grinding, the sound of a heavy stone vault lid sliding into place. Locks engage there too, sealing them inside their sarcophagus where they are safe.

Aleron and I are on the wrong side of every single lock

down here, I feel anything but safe. Although Lucius was kind enough to leave a light on in the other room, little of it reaches as far back as this small cell. I can make out enough to know this room has no furniture—no chair, no bed, no bucket to piss in, no food or water. Folding my legs under me, I sit down in naked dirt—ah, here it is, the source of the musty smell—with my arms folded around me for warmth. It's not as cold as Ignacio's underground tomb, but it's not exactly toasty warm, either.

"It's just one night," Aleron tells me, but he has no way of knowing that any more than I do. I just suspect he's wrong.

Moving behind me, he sighs as he lowers himself to sit with his back tucked up against the wall.

"Come here," he says, but I don't move. Wrapping his arm around my waist, he hauls me back against him. I try to resist him, but it's like trying to shrug off an octopus, and I'm just so tired. In the end, it's both easier and more comfortable to give in.

"I'm hungry," I mutter, feeling childish just for voicing it.

Aleron says nothing. He simply adjusts his coat around me so that I am as covered as I can be. Then, leaning back against the wall, he settles in to spend the night being my mattress as I lean sideways up against him. My knees drawn up to my chin, I rest my head against his chest and try to be so damned ungrateful.

It's a strange thing to be lying on someone whose heart doesn't beat and who only takes a breath when he's talking. He strokes my hair and my back. I love the way his hands feel, strong and calm, in spite of where we are.

"I'm sorry I wiped your mind," he says. When he strokes my hair again, it's all I can do not to smack his hand. "I know what I have taken from you must leave you feeling violated, but…"

"It does," I snap, then add "But I get it."

His hand stills on my back and he tips his head, as if he can see my face in the dark. Maybe he can, but all I see is just a ghost of paleness in ink-black air. I can't even make out his face. "You do?"

"Humans are panicky animals," I retort. "We don't like not knowing we're not the top of the food chain."

It's the snarkiest answer I can muster, and yet it feels hollow. If forced to be honest, I do kind of understand, and that makes it worse because when this is all over what's going to happen to me? Either I'll be dead, or I'm going to get my mind wiped again. How much will I lose this time? My sister's death? My sister in her entirety? Maybe it will just be everything that's happened to me since walking through Club Toxic's front door. Aleron saving my life… being chained in his bedroom… pressed up to the door with my hands bound by nothing but his verbal command not to move. His mouth on my clit, or on my neck as we waited in the dark on Ignacio's stone steps, with me bared to the cold while his hands brought me to the very edge of orgasm, over and over and over again.

And now here we are, in the dark once more, and I know I should be furious, but all I can think about is how good it felt with just the tip of his cock inside me, and how desperately I would do anything right now to feel him stroking deeper.

He tries to put his arms around me.

I elbow him in the ribs and shove at his hands, but as angry as I am inside, that's how much I wish he'd just hold me. A vampire. A killer.

I shiver, closing my mind so I won't see that by now familiar collage of visions pouring through my head.

My hands bound up on a bar with cuffs pulling me onto tiptoes while the shadow of him dressed only in pants moves behind me, combing out the tails of his flogger as he prepares to swing...

Me backed against the wallpaper somewhere in his house, holding his head as he bites and licks and loves between my thighs...

My whole body pulling taut as I come...

...as I shout to that first slow invasion of Aleron's cock forcing its way into my ass...

...as I writhe to the blows of his paddle, his hand, his flogger...

...his mouth kissing me, his teeth sinking in on the side of my neck, my wrist, my thighs, my pussy...

"Don't be frightened," he murmurs.

I'm shaking, but not because I'm scared and certainly not because I'm cold. My nipples are tight, swollen, heavy. Desperate for the attention of his mouth and the scrap of his teeth before he bites me there too, marking his territory.

"I'm scared; I'm pissed," I snap back, but if he can smell me half as well as I think he can, then he already knows that isn't true.

Are my dreams lying to me? They've come close, but nothing they've shown me yet has been exact.

Maybe these aren't visions at all. Maybe the things I'm

seeing are only what I hope for... a weird combination of what he's already done and what I know he's capable of. Maybe it's just daydreams of things I never knew I wanted until the night I met this man. But a part of me wants them now.

A part of me wants *him*.

Pulling out of his arms, I try to push away, but just that fast his hand in my hair seizes hold at the base of my scalp, pulling me sharply back against him.

"Let go!" I hiss, but he only lets me struggle until I've almost pried his fingers out of my hair. And then, suddenly, it's as if his patience—or perhaps it's simply his determination not to react—snaps.

Catching my ass in his hands, he lifts me all the way up off his lap. The next thing I know, my back is in the dirt and Aleron is above me. I grab his shoulders, but I don't have the will, much less the time, to push him back off again. Seizing my wrists, he pins them together in the soft earth above my head.

"Bound," he says, "by my will."

I want to hate him, but I can't. He tears his shirt in his haste to get his bare skin next to mine. Buttons go everywhere in the dirt and the dark as he rips my shirt straight down the middle. Then my breasts are in his hands, and my hands are still in the dirt where he ordered them to be. As mad as I am, I still want him. His mouth on my skin, hungrily kissing each nipple in turn before pressing a final kiss in between my breasts, as close as his mouth can come to my wildly beating heart. The muscular weight of his body pushing its way between thighs that aren't anywhere near as unwilling as they pretend to be.

I burn, despite the coolness of his flesh as he settles into the cradle of my legs. I wrap them both around him, needing him closer, but he's not leaving me. In jerks and tugs, he frees himself impatiently from his pants, shoving his trousers down far enough to be out of his way. And I keep my hands in the dirt, but I cling to him with both legs, digging my heels into the masculine curves of his ass just as he claps his hand over my mouth. There is no muffling my shout when he spears into me in a single, hard, soul-shattering thrust.

I'm not prepared, and yet I am so ready.

It hurts, but nothing has ever felt half as right or half as good as the breadth and the length of him forcibly filling me up.

He pushes in deep, pausing only when he can go no further, but I can't stop myself from bucking up to meet him, urging him that much deeper still.

I am burning for him, pulsing for him. Throbbing, aching, needing, gasping at the silken slide of his flesh slowly dragging back out of me, until I am sobbing his name over the exquisite brutality as his cock pushes deep once more.

He's not gentle, but he's everything I need him to be. I want to feel his ownership of me, not just now but hours from now. This feeling might be all I have left once they've wiped my mind.

I want to wear the bruises his hands leave on me as he grabs my shoulders and my thighs and rides me with vigorous thrusts. I beg him to bite me, and he must like the sound because he makes me plead, and whimper, and moan for it before I feel the blessed, claiming security of his fist seizing hold of my hair. Pulling my head sharply to one side, his thrusts become shorter, shallower, more frenzied as his other hand slides under my back, hooking two fingers deep into my ass at the same moment he bites. I come harder than I ever knew I could, with the pulsing wash of his cum spilling inside me, his fingers in my ass, and his name sobbing from my lips.

Eventually, the crashing, earth-shaking force of my orgasm dies away, leaving me trembling in his arms. His pumping thrusts dwindle and go still. His fingers retreat back out of me, so do his fangs. He licks, then kisses, then folds his arms around me, rolling me onto my side so he can curl up with me to sleep.

The last thing I hear before exhaustion and sleep take me is his whisper caressing behind my ear. "For better or worse, for richer or poorer. You belong to me now, Merris. You belong to me."

Then again, maybe I just dreamed it.

Aleron

I HATE SLEEPING IN DIRT, not just because it's filthy and I don't like not being clean, but because the musty smell of it pervades my senses and gives me nightmares.

I'm back in the grip of the one who sired me, with the pangs of this new hunger driving me into a frenzy of feeding that doesn't sate it. Only the blood of my new father can do that, and he gives it sparingly. One must earn the calm return to one's senses that supping from his veins will bring, but one only earns that through killing. So, out I go again, hunting among the hovels and the Crusader encampments that surround war-torn Antioch.

There are three of us and we all have the same command ringing in our ears. Only he with the highest body count will be fed on our return. We prove our count by collecting ears—the right one only—and our hunting ground is the armies our Father fears as much as he fears the sunlight he thinks they'll drag him into the longer this war continues. I kill without discrimination—Muslims, Turks, my own countrymen—it's a slaughter, and I'm good at it. Because night after night when the dawn forces our return, it's I who feeds gratefully from the vein our Father opens in his arm.

My brothers have been starved for weeks. Night after night they gorge on the hunting ground, but the blood they drink isn't Father's and makes them sick. Finally, they turn on us and I kill them too.

Eventually, I also kill Father. It's a fundamental truth of our kind: we all come to hate the one who makes us. I was still very much in my fledgling vampire youth the night I ripped Father's throat out. By rights, I never should have survived. They say only the strongest vampires can make others, and only the strongest of those survive the process. I should have died—God knows I screamed, writhed and begged for it in the days after he was dead. In the end, I proved strong enough. I lived.

All of that was a long time ago. I'm civilized now.

My eyes snap awake in the dark of a cell in Lucius's basement crypt. I've got visions of Father and his hunting ground still in my head, a familiar scent of danger and shifters in my nose, and Merris curled warm in my arms. I don't care how angry she is at me, I come up over the top of her feral as only one of my kind cornered can be just as the door to our cell rips open and shifters come pouring in.

There are more than a dozen of them, in both human as well as their massive wolf and smaller coyote forms. Merris screams as they tear into me in a full-on frenzy meant to overpower if not to kill.

The sun is still up. After almost nine hundred years, I don't need to see it to know night is not yet upon us. How they got to us, I don't know, but they've brought stakes. For me, and for Merris.

This is why you should never love someone.

Her scream is shrill and her small hands clutch at me in panic just before the coyote shifters rip her away. I grab after her, but they drag her from our prison cell by her arms and her hair. The bigger wolves tear at me, and I can't get out from under them to save her.

Her scream cuts off abruptly, and then the scent of her blood hits my nose.

I come up out of the middle of those ravening, mindless, fucking animals—kicking, punching, fighting my way out of the cell in time to see her lying face down on the floor. That white bitch, Selene is braced over the top of her, and I go mad.

I only thought I was civilized.

Now I'm going to kill them all.

And I'm going to start with her.

CHAPTER 12

$\mathcal{A}$*leron*

"S<small>TOP</small>!" someone shouts, but I barely hear it.

The shifter wolves attack with a vengeance, their teeth tearing into my arms and legs, but I barely feel it. I'm punching them, throwing them, fighting my way to the vampire-shifter abomination. She holds her ground, every hackle raised, snarling now right at me, but if I could have gotten my hands on her, I would have ripped the bitch apart.

It's Lucius in the end who stops me.

His rise to power did not happen by accident. He is far older than I am, by more than twice my years. He has the strength and the speed that only time can give my kind, but still I am intent. He has my throat and I have his. Our fangs are out. So are our claws. His blood is on my nails before the realization seeps in through my rage that both packs of shifters have pulled back and he is trying now to subdue me, not kill me.

"Stop!" Selene shouts. The white bitch has shifted back into her human form. I can barely make out the tiniest fumbling of motion from Merris underneath her.

She's protecting Merris. She's not trying to kill her. That knowledge seeps into me even more slowly, but still my fight is to get to her and I am trying.

Lucius is on my back now, his arm around my neck, using all his weight to hold on to me. The shifters are trying to hold me back too now. They grab my arms and legs, and the combined weight of them is stronger than I am. They force me to the floor, pinning me against the stones. But still I see only Merris, slowly pushing onto her hands and knees. When she touches the back of her head, her fingers come away bloody.

I would have killed every one of them all over again, if only I could get free.

"Do not," Lucius growls behind my ear, "make me kill you. Because I will."

But he won't be the first king I've killed. And so the battle lines are drawn.

Not that I can vocalize as much. Every thought I have, every fiber of my being, is locked on Merris as she pushes away from Selene. She could have run. She wouldn't get very far, but she doesn't even try. Instead, it's me that she comes crawling back to, and she does it punching and swearing, and tearing at shifters with her horribly ineffective, blunt human claws.

The shifters release me and scramble back. Lucius is more abrupt. He shoves off me, and we are two of kind. Old warriors both, with no thought but for the women we quickly snatch out of danger's way. Our movements both are blurred. He puts himself between me and his cautious queen—she is deadly in her own right, I can tell by her glare.

I grab Merris, kicking backwards across the floor until solid wall is at my back and all my enemies are now before me. She is trying to protect me, every bit as much as I strive to protect her.

"What. The *fuck*!" Lucius spits, casting the scope of his glare now out beyond just me. He scowls at the shifters now too, and I only know the alpha when the king locks eyes on him. "Garrett, get out of my house!"

"The house might be yours," the Alpha of the Tucson pack growls back, "but this city is ours."

"We had a truce—"

"Which you broke," another male shouts. The smaller coyote-shifter advances only until Garrett catches his shoulder. "You broke it the minute one of your kind killed my grandmother!"

"It was *not* one of mine!" Catching himself, Lucius visibly struggles to contain his anger. I know how he feels. I've got Merris tucked behind me. Her hands clutch my shoulder. Her blood is in my nose and my veins, and all I want is vengeance against every shifter in this room. I don't much care for the species under the best of circumstances. Right now, I would dearly love to murder them all. "I told you I'd handle it and I will."

"When?" Garrett snaps. "When you get around to it? After you've had your little nap?"

"When I know something!" Lucius snaps back, advancing on the Alpha wolf-shifter, a single step that riles every shifter packed in this basement.

It's Selene who announces, "She didn't do it." Turning to Garrett, very quietly she says, "You know me. I wouldn't protect her if I thought for a second she had. But there was no trace of the matriarch's smell on her when they arrived this morning, and she's not a vampire." Turning to the much younger Camino Seco coyote Alpha, she adds, "What was done to your grandmother, you know a human isn't responsible for. You *know* it."

The male holds her stare, fury and grief waging their silent war in the minute flinches of his expression. In the end, he looks away first, looking straight at Merris instead. I keep her tucked behind me. If he makes one move toward us, I will tear him open from gut to throat. But the white queen is right. He does know, only his rage needs a victim and he doesn't want to believe it.

"I will find the vampire responsible," Lucius tells them, soft in spite of his anger. "I have given you my word."

"We will eradicate every vampire in this city if you don't," the Alpha wolf replies. It's not an ill-thought out threat, either. He believes he can do it, Lucius believes he will try, and after what happened here now, as much as I am loathe to admit it, I believe he might even succeed.

Perhaps that's why I am finally able to swallow past the fury still choking me enough to say one name. "Athanasius."

They all look at me.

I forgive none of them, nor will I ever.

"He goes by Arthur now," Merris says dryly, holding me with one hand and touching the back of her head. Though the bleeding has stopped, she's still checking her fingers, and I'm sure her head must hurt.

"Who?" Lucius asks.

"Arthur, Athanasius," I repeat both names. It's all I can do to keep a civil tone. "He's a drug addict who's trying to take Club Toxic as his new hunting ground. Unfortunately, he killed a girl."

"Jez," Merris supplies. "My sister."

"Merris came to the nightclub and, mistaking her for Jez, he panicked. Afraid she might alert Lucius to his presence, he tried to kill her, first at the nightclub—"

"The shooting," Lucius says, gleaning the missing pieces to his own mental puzzle.

"—and then again at Merris's apartment complex." I look to the Camino Seco coyote Alpha. He still has a stake meant either for Merris or for me in his hand, and I harbor not an ounce of sympathy for the naked grief I can see in his eyes. "As near as I can figure, considering his mood when we got there, he killed your grandmother and everyone else in the building simply because he could."

"Athanasius," Garrett, the more powerful Alpha wolfshifter repeats, saying the name as if it also came with a scent he could carry in his nose.

"He goes by Arthur now." I'm imagining how good it will feel to hunt every one of these animals down.

"I will find him," Lucius promises.

"Only if we don't find him first," Garrett replies. "You

still have six hours until sunset. Frankly, the only reason we decided to come down here, instead of burning the house down around you, was out of respect to your mate. We'll find 'Arthur'. We'll rout his entire God-damn nest. Consider this your first, last, and only warning. The next time one of your kind decides to treat mine as wasted meat, the truce is over. I'll drag every last one of you motherfuckers out into the sun."

The shifters withdraw back up the basement steps, leaving Lucius and his vampire-shifter queen exchanging uneasy glances.

"I'm sorry," he tells me once they are gone, but he doesn't trust me, and I don't forgive him. We have no choice but to return to our cell, Merris and I, and once more he locks our prison door.

"I'm sorry I got you into this," she whispers, but only after the rocky grind of the stone sarcophagus lid slides shut, signaling Lucius and his mate have returned to their sleep.

She tries to hold me, and I hold her back but I do so sitting in the dirt in front of the door. Eventually, the darkness takes its toll on her. She's only human, and she's tired. She sleeps, curled up in my lap with her head on my shoulder and her soft breath warming the skin above my collar.

I don't close my eyes. This is the last time I'll ever rest in an enemy's lair.

I may never sleep easily again.

∼

Merris

THE SOUND of the door opening startles me awake. I come upright with a shout and a slap, but Aleron is already up. I don't know when he moved me from his lap to the floor, or maybe he never did. Maybe he stood up just that fast, flashing the way he sometimes does, faster than my eyes can follow. But he's standing between me and the door before I can do more than realize it's Lucius standing there, not the wolf-people coming back to finish us off.

Wolf-people? Coyote-people. W*ere-whatevers*.

I guess now I know what shifters are.

Contrary to what the movies suggest, the world of paranormal beings is not one giant, happy family. They do not like one another. They do *not* get along.

"We don't have a lot of time," Lucius says, holding the door open. "We're going to have to hurry if we want to clean this mess up ourselves."

I scramble to my feet, more than ready to get out of this cell, but Aleron stays me with his hand.

"Happy hunting," he tells the other vampire.

I'm getting really, really good at reading vampire expressions. I swear I glimpse a flash of anger move through the king's eyes. "You feel no obligation to help?"

"Whatever obligation I felt died six hours ago when her blood hit your floor."

I touch his arm. "I'm okay."

Those few moments in the darkness when the door wrenched open and the wolves came snarling in, those were the scariest I think I've ever known. I was bitten three times, but not savaged. I'm stiff right now, a little sore—particularly around the bites on my ankle, arm and the knee of my other leg, where they'd grabbed and dragged me out of the cell. And of course, the back of my head where I got hit. I've no idea with what, but that blow sent me sprawling face first on the floor. Had Selene not thrown herself into the fight to protect me, I have no doubt I'd have been killed.

But she did protect me.

So did Aleron.

Whatever anger I'd been feeling earlier, it's gone. All I want to do now is get the hell out of here. Leave. Get in Aleron's car and have him drive as far and as fast he wants to go, but Lucius is right. This is all far from over. Vampires are trying to kill me, shifters hate me, and my own people think I'm responsible for a mass murder, and no one's mind-wiped me yet. There's no escape for me yet, not in any direction. But after last night, I do know one thing. When Aleron comes to wipe my memories, I'm going to let him. It's not that I want to forget. As awful as parts of this have been, I would do anything to keep my memories of Aleron. But now I can see just how much of a risk he's taking for me. The last thing I want is for him to get hurt because I was being selfish.

"I'll find you some clothes," Selene says, heading for the stairs. When we reach the top, she heads off in one direction, but I'm more concerned with finding something to eat and drink, and I'm not at all shy about raiding their kitchen to do it. I shouldn't be surprised to find blood in the refrigerator, but they've recently celebrated with a dinner out, because I find takeout ribs and half of a baked sweet potato in a Styrofoam box.

"Help yourself," Lucius says dryly, but by then I'm standing over the sink with a partially devoured sweet potato in one hand and I'm rapidly gnawing the meat off a rib bone in my other. My mouth is stuffed too full to answer. I just keep chewing.

It's a few minutes after that, that Selene calls for her mate from another part of the house. Her voice is strange, just strained enough to bring us all following the sound until we find her standing in the front entryway, staring through drapes that had been closed last night but now stand wide open. The view overlooks their front yard and driveway all the way back to the entry gate that stands closed to keep out uninvited guests.

It's a metal gate, with the bars fashioned into decorative spikes across the top. In a ghastly row speared atop some of those spikes are seven blackened masses. They look like pumpkins at first glance, charred almost to crumbling into dust, with hair of varying colors and lengths and indents that look like mouths gaping open in silent screams. The shoulder-length brown strands of one are long enough to catch in the faint night wind. It billows sideways and as it does, I can see bits of char turning to dust and blowing away.

"What is that?" I hear myself ask, my own voice sounding strange from the shock of what I was seeing.

"Garrett left us a message." Lucius opens the door and he, Aleron, and even Selene head down the driveway for a closer look. I don't go with them. I don't want to see those pumpkins turning into faces, all blackened, burned and screaming, and slowly crumbling into ash with each puff of wind that rustles through their hair.

Approaching one, Aleron reaches up to take it off the gate and the entire form simply crumbles in a billow of drifting ash and small bits of bone that rain down through the bars of the gate. Only a few of the others do the same. The rest lose their flesh in drifting gray and black clouds that scatter across the mouth of the driveway in the bright glow of the yard lights. The skulls remain.

"Let's get you dressed," Selene says, coming back up to the house.

I don't move. "Is… is that Athanasius?"

"And his nest, from the looks of it." She looks at me with such an absence of sympathy. As if she takes heads off her gate all the time. I can't even imagine.

"They tortured them, didn't they?" Rooted in the doorway, I feel sick as I watch Lucius and Aleron take down the heads.

"No," she answers. "They cut their heads off, yes. But what you're seeing is what happens to vampires exposed to the sun. It's a warning."

"Play nice or else?"

"This is shifter territory. Lucius buffaloed his way in, making a place for himself and Club Toxic, but he doesn't control Tucson. This is just a reminder." She glances back over her shoulder at her mate, coming back up the driveway with an armful of skulls and skull pieces. "Shifters have been mistreated by vampires for centuries. Lucius is trying to change that, but even so, this is Garrett's way of saying he's all done taking it."

Aleron is trailing along behind Lucius, carrying more

skulls. His gaze finds mine. It's weird, how the yard lights seem to catch in his eyes, making them glow like a predator's.

"Do you want a shower?"

"Please." I shiver, unaware that my hand has drifted up to touch the tender place where he bit me. My nipples tighten, the peaks of them already aching for his next kiss.

CHAPTER 13

leron

"Do you want help?" Lucius asks as we dump the skulls of those vampires too recently turned for the sunlight to destroy completely in the flowerbed behind the garbage cans. He'll need to dispose of them later, but he's king of his nest. Supposedly, he has those he can command to do that for him. Either way, I still have problems of my own to clean up, so I'll not be volunteering.

The question, however, does catch me off-guard.

"You mean the police station?" I ask, because frankly, that's what I've been thinking about.

Athanasius was the first head I tried to touch down on that gate. I recognized him by his hair. One problem solved, but the human one remains. Merris will continue to be hunted by her own people until the mass murder is solved—unlikely, since the man responsible is now ash in

207

the wind—or until I walk into the appropriate police station and compel everyone there to wipe her from their investigation. As much as I'd love to tell him where he can stick it, I consider his offer carefully.

"Perhaps. I've never tried to affect that many minds at once. It won't just be mind-wiping, however. We'll need to get them to erase her from the computer files and any report she might appear in. It might just be easier to convince them all she's dead."

"Probably," Lucius agrees. "But while I am happy to help remove her from the investigation, that isn't what I meant."

Brushing the dust off my hands and the front of my now quite dirty trousers—lord, the state of me—I give him only half an ear. "What do you mean?"

"You were willing to allow yourself to be torn to pieces to protect that girl last night. A girl who knows of our existence and who, apart from everything else, now knows where I live. May I ask, what are your intentions?"

I have zero interest in discussing my intimate feelings with a man who threw both me and Merris to the shifters, not to mention keeping us locked in his cell all night.

"Don't worry," I promise. "After tonight, I intend to take her as far from this place as any two people can possibly get. You'll never find her much less hurt her again."

"Are you bonded?" he softly asks.

"Go fuck yourself," I return in kind.

He doesn't appear at all offended. If anything, he seems sympathetic. "I have sired many vampires. I don't know if you've yet tried, but if that is what you want for her, I would be willing to help. There are always risks, but if she's strong enough to survive the process, then I will do everything I can. I promise, I will not be cruel and will release her to you as soon as I can."

I stare at him. Honestly, I don't know whether to be touched by his offer or infuriated by it. "What makes you think that is something I would ever do to someone I love?"

He seems surprised. "What alternative do you have?"

I move in close to him, just upset enough not to care if he perceives it to be a threat. Vampires have killed one another for less, but I am beyond calculating the consequences. "I will hold her every day for the rest of her life, however long that may be. I will watch over her until the day she draws her last breath, and between this moment and that, do everything in my power to ensure she never has reason to doubt my affection. And yes, one day I will have to let her go, but I would sooner stand at her gravesite and watch the sun come up than to spend the next hundred years watching what love she bears for me slowly die as she realizes exactly what I've done to her."

"It doesn't have to be that way," he tries to say, but I cut him off with another step.

"When have you ever found it not to end that way? Tell me, which of your sired has not come to hate you in the end?"

Lucius stares at me, but he doesn't answer.

"Thank you for your offer, but I believe I will decline." I back from him. "Good luck to you and your shifter queen."

He frowns, but I don't care. I walk back into his house

in search of my Merris and find her in a steamy bathroom, taking a shower. I miss being clean. I miss the touch of her skin on mine even more.

I should leave. Give her this one last moment of privacy before I spring it on her that I'm taking her away from this city, state, and perhaps even the continent. Never to return, at least until I'm sure she'll be safe.

But I can't make myself go. I come all the way inside, shutting and locking the door behind me.

I don't know if it's the click of the lock she hears or if she spies my motions through the steam-covered glass. Either way, she stops in the middle of washing her hair and pokes her head out the door. I shouldn't be surprised that she's beautiful wet, with her hair slicked down and her eyelashes all clumped together, but she gives me a worried moment to spring more bad news on her. When it doesn't come, the worry melts into understanding, regret, and finally sadness.

"Are you going to wipe my mind now?" She doesn't look at me, but I can tell she's steeling herself to go through with it without protest. My darling Merris.

I shake my head. "I'm not going to wipe your mind."

She looks up, and at first, she doesn't look any happier to hear that. "B-but... the risk to you is—"

"My decision is final," I say gently, but firmly. "Besides, I would much rather take you with me, then I would wipe your mind and leave you behind. I would happily take you anywhere in the world you'd like to go. You could practice your art, visit the finest museums." I do my best to make running for our lives sound appealing. "Whatever I need to do to keep you safe, believe me, I will do it. Merris, I… I will do anything to keep you with me. Of course, you can say no if you'd rather stay here. The decision of whether or not to wipe your mind won't be mine any longer, but I will still do whatever is required to make sure you are—"

"I'll go with you," she softly interrupts.

"—as safe as I possibly—"

"I'll go with you," she says again, when it suddenly hits me what she's just agreed to. Of the two of us, I got the better end of this deal by far. I'm not used to being so thoroughly humbled. I have no idea what to say.

Opening the shower door a little wider, she shyly asks, "D-do you want some of this hot water before I take it all?"

It's not the water I crave, but I strip down and step in behind her. The spray hits me, hot against my skin, warming me slowly although I still feel her startle when I touch her. She laughs, but it's a faltering awkward sound. She's trying not to look at me, but she can't seem to help herself. It's the first time she's seen me in the light. Her gaze goes right to my cock. She could not have made me harder had she cupped my balls and stroked me in her wet, soapy hand.

She laughs even more awkwardly and quickly looks away, but not before I see the flush of pink darken in her cheeks and the stiffening of her nipples as they rise into dusky peaks. The steam carries her scent, but I have only to part the folds of her sex to spice the air with her arousal. She is wet, and soapy, but it only takes a caress of my finger to make her turn back toward me.

"I miss my gloves," I say, just before she catches the back of my neck and pulls me hungrily into her kiss.

We have a lot to do tonight. I need to collect money, travel documents, clothes... for me and for her. I'll get her a new identity and take her somewhere safe. I have many houses scattered around the globe, all of them guarded by someone like Consuela, content to collect a paycheck in my absence and ask no questions. Wherever we end up, I'll have to bring my cars over one at a time, but we won't return to Tucson. Not in her lifetime, maybe never again in mine.

I'm surprised how little that bothers me, but the only thing that can't be replaced is what I am holding now in my arms. Backing her slowly up against the shower wall, I take her hands in mine and pin them to the tiles above her head.

"I'm sorry," she whispers, shivering. "I'm sorry for what I said last night. I was upset and I took it out on you, and I'm sorry..."

I touch a finger to her lips, caressing the bottommost with my thumb as she stammers to silence. "I bear you no grudges."

Goosebumps break out all over her, a trail of desire that I read with my lips and my fingertips all the way down the plane of her flinching belly to the softness of her mons. Her sex is deliciously bare, every perfect fold ready for my inspection.

Her breath catches when I part her open between my thumbs. Her clit and labia are swelling, eager to be touched, licked, kissed. Bit.

Owned. By me.

Only by me.

Forever by me.

"I love you, Merris," I tell her, lowering myself to kneel in the bottom of the shower, with the hot water beating down upon my back and her pussy splayed open and waiting for my first kiss.

She swallows convulsively. "I love you too," she whispers back. Her eyes show how much that scares her, and yet too do they betray how much she means it. And all that even before I caress her with my fingers and lean in for that first delicious kiss.

She grabs her own hair—obedient submissive that she is just learning how to be. Her gasp is sharp as she fights herself to hold as still as possible. There is no sight half as beautiful as the heaving of her breasts as she strives not to arch, or the quivering that quickly takes hold of her thighs as I lash and lick, and eventually drape her thigh over my shoulder so I can get all the way in to drink the sweet nectar her pussy can't stop weeping. For me.

Her body is mine and I adore it. Every trembling curve, every hidden vale.

I bring her right to the cusp of coming, when her shaking is at its most intense and every breath she exhales is just a shade shy of becoming a moan or cry. That's when at last I stand, grab her by her ass and her thighs and heft her all the way up so I might drink the cries she makes straight from her lips when I enter her.

Mine.

I try to be gentle with her. I have spent the last five hundred years learning how to be civilized. The shifters dashed all of that to nothing when they tried to take her from me in the basement. Merris dashes it all over again when the blunted tips of her all-too-human teeth catch my bottom lip in a nipping bite.

My knee-jerk reaction is as savage as the warning growl that rolls up out of me. "Merris…"

Clinging to my shoulders, her legs wrapping tight around my waist, she throws her head back with a breathy laugh, not only accepting the force with which my hips now slap into hers, but exalting in it. I could have broken the wall with her, in the mood that husky laugh of hers put me in. But I try to rein it in. I try to be gentle.

If only she didn't bow her head to mine and, in that hot breath of challenge, whisper, "Now who's bound to whom?"

I think I have been almost from the moment that we met.

But I'll never tell her that.

She nips the side of my neck, and I yank her off the tile wall, dropping her down into the bottom of that spacious shower. There isn't an ounce of hot water left in Lucius's pipes or so much as a rasp of voice left in my darling Merris's cries by the time I'm through.

It's hard to feel badly about that. After all, I am the Master.

I'm the only one who bites.

The End

WANT MORE?

et ready for the next book in the Midnight Doms series, *Her Vampire Prince* by Ines Johnson.

HER VAMPIRE PRINCE (MIDNIGHT DOMS, Book 2)

Cari

How hard is it to die? Don't ask me. I've been failing at it for a year.

My father lost his life in a fatal car wreck while I walked away without a scratch. Now I taunt that bastard Death on a daily basis. Volcano hopping. Street racing. Skydiving. But then Death comes for me.

Hadrian

For centuries, I've been a dead vampire walking. No warmth, no feeling. No reason to live.

Then she bursts into my life. A mortal daredevil with a

carefree laugh. She literally falls from the sky and into my arms. She's got a death wish and I've got a hunger only she can slake.

She's my prey, but she wants to leave?
No way. She's mine. And I'm never letting her go.
—> ORDER NOW

-JOIN OUR FACEBOOK PARTY ROOM: https://www.facebook.com/groups/701925946969115/

—SIGN up to get news of the Midnight Doms releases: https://www.subscribepage.com/midnightdoms

ABOUT MAREN SMITH

Fortunate enough to live with my Daddy Dom, I am a Little, coffee fanatic, was administrator at my local BDSM dungeon for more than six years, am a resident of the wilds of freakin' Kansas (still don't know how I ended up here) and submissive to the love of my life. An International and USA Bestselling Author, I have penned more than 160 novels, novellas and short stories, and am the author of the Masters of the Castle series.

Want information on free stories, new releases, takeovers, giveaways and prizes? Join my newsletter! http://MarenSmith.com/newsletter/

Get the latest on sales and special release pricing by following me on Bookbub! https://www.bookbub.com/profile/maren-smith

If you enjoyed this story, try these:
  Her Montana Master
  Fearless (Black Light, Book 10)

READ THE BAD BOY ALPHA SERIES
THAT LAUNCHED MIDNIGHT DOMS

Bad Boy Alphas Series
Alpha's Temptation
Alpha's Danger
Alpha's Prize
Alpha's Challenge
Alpha's Obsession
Alpha's Desire
Alpha's War
Alpha's Mission
Alpha's Bane
Alpha's Secret
Alpha's Prey
Alpha's Blood
Alpha's Sun